**The only way for Miguel to guarantee she'd be safe would be to stay here himself.**

Suddenly she turned to look at him and beamed an unexpected smile in his direction. The worry in her face disappeared. Her blue eyes shimmered like sunlight on a mountain lake.

The analytical side of his brain shut down. As he stared at her, he forgot the potential danger that had brought him here.

For just a minute, he almost felt like they were on a date.

"Thank you for coming over here so quickly tonight."

"My pleasure." Earlier he'd been thinking he should stay at her house as a bodyguard. Now he had another reason altogether. He *wanted* to be here, *wanted* to be with her.

"I should get going to the café, pick up that order."

Shyly, she bit her lower lip, then said, "Hurry back."

And those words gave him every reason to want to.

# CASSIE MILES

# CRIMINALLY HANDSOME

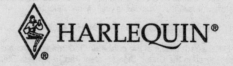

TORONTO • NEW YORK • LONDON
AMSTERDAM • PARIS • SYDNEY • HAMBURG
STOCKHOLM • ATHENS • TOKYO • MILAN • MADRID
PRAGUE • WARSAW • BUDAPEST • AUCKLAND

Special thanks and acknowledgment
to Cassie Miles for her contribution to
the Kenner County Crime Unit miniseries.

Recycling programs
for this product may
not exist in your area.

ISBN-13: 978-0-373-69393-1
ISBN-10:  0-373-69393-1

CRIMINALLY HANDSOME

Copyright © 2009 by Harlequin Books S.A.

**Printed in U.S.A.**

## ABOUT THE AUTHOR

Though born in Chicago and raised in L.A., Cassie Miles has lived in Colorado long enough to be considered a seminative. The first home she owned was a log cabin in the mountains overlooking Elk Creek with a thirty-mile commute to her work at the *Denver Post*.

After raising two daughters and cooking tons of macaroni and cheese for her family, Cassie is trying to be more adventurous in her culinary efforts. Ceviche, anyone? She's discovered that almost anything tastes better with wine. A lot of wine. When she's not plotting Harlequin Intrigue books, Cassie likes to hang out at the Denver Botanical Gardens near her high-rise home.

### Books by Cassie Miles

HARLEQUIN INTRIGUE
874—WARRIOR SPIRIT
904—UNDERCOVER COLORADO**
910—MURDER ON THE MOUNTAIN**
948—FOOTPRINTS IN THE SNOW
978—PROTECTIVE CONFINEMENT†
984—COMPROMISED SECURITY†
999—NAVAJO ECHOES
1025—CHRISTMAS COVER-UP
1048—MYSTERIOUS MILLIONAIRE
1074—IN THE MANOR WITH THE MILLIONAIRE
1102—CHRISTMAS CRIME IN COLORADO
1126—CRIMINALLY HANDSOME

**Rocky Mountain Safe House
†Safe House: Mesa Verde

# CAST OF CHARACTERS

*Emma Richardson*—A psychic medium whose visions may lead to solving the crime or to lethal danger.

*Miguel Acevedo*—A forensic scientist specializing in crime scene analysis and rational thinking.

*Aspen Meadows*—Emma's cousin who disappeared under mysterious circumstances.

*Jack Meadows*—Aspen's infant son.

*Aunt Rose and Grandma Quinn*—Emma's relatives who visit from the other side.

*Dylan Acevedo*—An FBI agent, twin brother of Miguel.

*Callie MacBride*—Head of the Kenner County Crime Lab.

*Patrick Martinez*—Sheriff of Kenner County.

*Bree Hunter*—Detective at the Ute Reservation.

*Julie Grainger*—Murdered FBI agent.

*Vincent Del Gardo*—Las Vegas crime boss, suspected in Julie's murder.

*Boyd Perkins*—Hitman from Vegas.

*Sherman Watts*—The evidence connects him to Aspen's disappearance.

*Hank Bridger*—A Las Vegas thug who wants to collect a debt from Del Gardo.

# *Chapter One*

Emma Richardson folded her arms on the desktop in her home office and laid down her head. At nine o'clock in the morning, it was too early for a nap. But she was tired, so very tired.

*I'll only rest my eyes. Only for a moment. While the house is quiet....*

Reality faded as a psychic vision seeped into her mind. Daylight shimmered and vanished, transformed into night.

She was in a forest.

A cold wind rattled through bare branches, and the shadows shifted beneath her feet. Beside her, to the east, the dark waters of a wide, wild river crashed against rocks and boulders, spewing a deadly froth.

A tall woman appeared. She wore an FBI jacket. Her eyes were hollow. Her lips were white and dead. She spoke only one word. "Run."

Emma didn't ask why. She knew. He was coming closer. The danger was coming closer.

She scrambled over the rocks at the river's edge. This was no good; she needed to seek open ground. Turning to the west, she fought her way through thicket, pine and cottonwood. The trees dissuaded her. West was the wrong direction. On the medicine wheel, west meant death.

She slipped, caught hold of the slender white trunk of an aspen. The bark felt warm, full of life. The branches were green with leaves. This tree had saved her balance, kept her from falling.

With a final effort, she crawled into the open. As she ran, her sneakers dug into the moist earth, still saturated from the recent blizzard. She vaulted over low shrubs and patches of snow, running hard, running for her life.

The muscles in her thighs throbbed. Her blood pumped so fiercely through her veins that her ears were ringing. But she had to keep going. If she stopped, he'd catch her.

Straight ahead, she saw a car, and she heard the cries of an infant. She had to protect him. She veered toward the south—the direction of safety—leading her pursuer away from the precious child.

He was gaining. So close that she felt his hot, fetid breath on the back of her neck. His hands grabbed her jacket. There was no escape. He had her. She fell.

He was on top of her. Shadows hid his face but she saw his necklace. A leather medallion with a black bear claw design. He held a knife. Moonlight gleamed on the silver blade.

Through the ringing in her ears, she heard him say, "Aspen got away. But you will die."

As the blade descended toward her throat, her eyelids closed....

She woke with a start, jolted back in the swivel chair. April sunlight poured through the window. The screen saver on her computer showed a random lightning bolt pattern. Though Emma knew she was safe at home, the aura of danger lingered. Her heart raced as if she had actually been running.

Finally, she'd had a vision. Finally, her gift as a medium might help her find her cousin.

Before the images faded in her memory, she grabbed a piece of paper and wrote down all that she could remember. Her pen flew across the page, making sketchy notes: Woman in FBI jacket. The river to the east. The green aspen leaves. Running to the west. The car with the baby. Turn to the south. His knife. His leather necklace. She drew the bear claw design.

Lifting her pen, she looked down at the paper and saw that she'd unintentionally drawn a second design. Leafy with vines, it looked like a logo. Three letters twined together. VDG.

*Where did that come from?* And what did VDG stand for? Very Damn Good? Vines Do Grow? Or the *V* could stand for Virgin. She winced. *Don't go there.* This vision wasn't about her personal life. These images pertained to the disappearance of her cousin, Aspen Meadows.

*Aspen.* She circled the word. The aspen tree in her vision was leafy and warm, still flowing with sap. And the pursuer said that Aspen got away. Emma wanted to believe those words, wanted to believe that her cousin had survived the attack. But where was she?

Five weeks ago, just before a spring blizzard blanketed the southeast corner of Colorado with several feet of snow, Aspen's car had been found in a ditch just outside Kenner City. Her six-week-old son, Jack, was safe in his car seat, but Sheriff Patrick Martinez suspected foul play. When he placed Jack in Emma's care, he had warned her to be prepared for the worst.

But that couldn't be. Aspen wasn't dead. Whenever someone close to Emma passed on, she knew. The dead came to her from the other side, spoke to her, showed her visions or symbols. Ever since she was ten years old and her deceased grandmother warned her about the fire, she'd been a medium—able to communicate with the dead. At age thirty, she trusted her spirit visions almost more than reality.

For five long weeks, she'd been hoping that her psychic senses would give her a clue to Aspen's whereabouts, but nothing had come into her mind. Until now. The spirit who showed her this vision had to be the tall FBI woman—a dead woman. Who was she? How was she connected to Aspen's disappearance?

Emma closed her eyes and concentrated. *Who are you?*

Nothing came. Not a sound. Not a symbol.

*Please tell me. Who are you?*

Still nothing.

*Are your initials VDG?*

She heard a faint echo. *Julie.* Then silence again.

"Okay," Emma said as she opened her eyes. "Your name is Julie."

It was a start. Sometimes, Emma was able to reach out to these spirits, and they'd respond. She communicated often with her grandma Quinn and her aunt Rose, both of whom had been popping in to offer advice on how to care for Aspen's infant son. They observed and commented and nagged about how Emma was doing everything all wrong. If the spirits of Grandma and Aunt Rose had been able to change diapers, life would be so much easier. But no. Emma was the sole caregiver. Definitely not a job she'd signed up for.

She figured that the main reason she hadn't had a vision about Aspen's disappearance was severe sleep deprivation from baby Jack's every-few-hours feeding schedule. He was a cuddly little bundle of stringent demands: Feed me. Change me. Carry me. Rock me. Dealing with an infant was far more time-intensive than she'd ever imagined. Also, she had to admit, more rewarding.

Though she learned—from the dozens of baby care

books she'd purchased online—that Jack's change of facial expression could be nothing more than a reflex or a muscle twitch, his smile was amazing. And the random sounds he made—other than the full-throated crying—tickled her. In his wide-open eyes, she saw the wisdom of the ages. She had to find Aspen, to reunite her with this little miracle named Jack.

Finally, she had a vision to work with. Emma grabbed the phone on the desk and punched in the number for Sheriff Martinez. He owed her for a couple of cases where she'd used her skill as a medium to help him find missing persons. Now, it was his turn to help her.

MIGUEL ACEVEDO, a forensic investigator for the Kenner County Crime Lab, rode in the passenger seat beside Sheriff Patrick Martinez. Miguel hated that his analysis of a crime scene was being called into question. By a psychic? "This is a waste of time, my friend."

"Don't be so sure," Patrick said. "Over the years, Emma has helped with missing person cases. She's saved lives. Everybody around here trusts her and knows she's not a fraud."

"Why haven't I heard of her?"

"You don't know much about Kenner City. Your crime lab has only been here for a year."

Though the Four Corners area covered a huge territory in four different states, the small-town populations were insular. The people in Kenner City were slow to accept change, even slower to warm up to strangers. Miguel hardly knew anyone outside law enforcement. "Tell me about one of her cases."

"Remember last fall when that boy disappeared from his mother's house? Emma told me where to look."

"The boy was with his father." And it didn't take a visionary to figure out that the estranged dad snatched his own son. "Wasn't he your first suspect?"

"You bet, but Emma said they were in Durango. In a room with a wagon wheel in front. And she saw the number seven."

"Was she right?"

"Close enough. The name of the motel was the Covered Wagon. And it was room seventeen." Patrick reached up to adjust the brim of his Stetson. "Trust me. She's the real deal."

"A real psychic. Those two words are opposites. If something is real—as in reality—how can it be psychic?"

"You're a real pain in the ass, Miguel."

"It's my *primo* talent."

"And she's not really a psychic. She's a medium."

"What's the difference?"

"She talks to dead people."

*"Muy loco."* He lowered the window and pushed his open palm against the wind. A fresh coolness rushed inside the cuff of his denim jacket and plaid cotton shirt. A few weeks after the blizzard, there were still patches of snow on the shady side of the street and at the curbs where the snow plows had piled up little mountains. Today's temperature was already in the fifties. By noon, it would be sixty. The weather felt like spring. His favorite season. He felt like a kid instead of a thirty-three-year-old man, felt like he should stick his head out the window like a collie and let the wind blow through his hair.

He ran his fingers through that thick, black hair which was seriously in need of a trim, then turned toward Patrick. "Tell me, my friend. Did Emma the fortune teller predict that you'd fall in love with Bree Hunter?"

At the mention of his fiancée's name, the big tough sheriff melted like chocolate in *mole*. "Emma isn't that kind of psychic. She doesn't read a crystal ball."

"Exactly what kind of *bruja* is she?"

"She's not a witch," Patrick said. "There are scientific theories about paranormal abilities and mediums. Why are you so threatened?"

"She's no threat. Just a waste of my time."

He'd already done a thorough analysis of the vehicle abandoned by Aspen Meadows. From the skid marks left by tires and a high-impact dent on the rear bumper, he determined that Aspen's car was forced off the road into a shallow ditch. He'd found no fingerprints or other trace evidence in the car, other than those of Aspen and a few close friends, which led him to believe that she'd climbed out from behind the steering wheel and took off running— probably searching for help or trying to divert her pursuer from harming her baby.

Then Aspen disappeared. She was either purposely in hiding or dead. No matter what Emma Richardson said.

Patrick cleared his throat. "Do me a favor. Don't tease Emma."

"Why not? The *bruja* is sensitive?"

"Aspen is her cousin. They're close. They grew up together on the rez."

The nearby Ute Mountain Ute reservation took up thousands of acres on these high plains. Patrick's fiancée, Bree, was a detective on the tribal police force. "I didn't know Emma was Ute."

"Partly. She doesn't look it. Her hair is brown, not black. Her eyes are blue."

It must have been tough to live on the rez and not look like everybody else. Miguel would have felt a twinge of sympathy if he hadn't thought this whole psychic thing was crazy. "I won't give her a hard time, unless she asks for it."

"She's a good woman. When I told her about Aspen's disappearance, Emma stepped up and took responsibility. She's the temporary guardian for Aspen's baby."

"What about the father?"

"Aspen never said who he was."

"We could run the baby's DNA," Miguel said. "The father might be in the database."

"The guy obviously doesn't care. Baby Jack is better off with Emma."

The sheriff pulled into the driveway of a pretty little ranch-style house, white with black trim and a shake roof. The lot was huge and well-landscaped with indigenous pines and spruce. Empty flower boxes at the windows waited for their spring planting.

"Nice place." The cleanliness and normality surprised him. He'd halfway expected a haunted house with cobwebs draped across the windows and a graveyard in the back. "What does this medium do to earn her living?"

"Some kind of consulting or editing. She works at home on her computer." Patrick issued one last warning. "Be nice."

"I'll be on my best behavior, and that's saying a lot. I used to be an altar boy."

Like that churchgoing boy from so many years ago, he trudged along the sidewalk, dragging his feet. He'd rather be somewhere else. Back at the lab, he had work piling up and a new piece of audio analysis equipment he wanted to play with. He waited on the front stoop while Patrick rang the bell. From inside, he could hear a baby crying, which didn't exactly reassure him about Emma being a good mother substitute.

The door swung open. Miguel found himself staring into the huge blue eyes of a slender woman with straight, silky brown hair that fell across her forehead and was cut in a straight line at her sharp, little chin. He saw hints of her Ute heritage in her dusky complexion and high cheekbones. Her lips pulled into a wide, open smile as she greeted Patrick. Though she balanced the fussing baby in her arms, she managed to shake his hand when the sheriff introduced them.

"Pleased to meet you, Miguel."

"Same here."

His first impression was all good, *muy bueno*. As he entered her house, he studied her more closely. As a CSI, he was trained to notice details. Her silver earrings and the necklace around her long, slender neck had a distinctive Ute design. Her beige turtleneck, almost the same color as her skin, and her jeans resembled the typical outfit worn by most people in the area at this time of year. But the fabric of her turtleneck was silk. He didn't know much about women's clothing, but he suspected that she shopped in classy boutiques.

In her sunlit kitchen, she offered them coffee.

With a glance at Miguel, Patrick said, "We probably shouldn't waste any time."

"No rush," Miguel said.

"Oh, good," Emma said as she bounced up and down with the whimpering baby, gently stroking the fine hair on top of his head. "Because it's time for Jack's feeding. I just finished heating the formula."

"I'll take the baby."

Miguel held out his arms. Back home, he had a growing herd of nieces and nephews. Though his family lived only a few hours' drive away from Kenner City, his schedule didn't leave much time for visits, and he missed them.

When she handed over the baby, dressed in footed pajamas, he wrapped the blanket snugly around the infant's tiny legs and cradled him in the crook of his arm. "Hush, *mijo*."

The baby looked toward him. As soon as Miguel took a seat at the kitchen table, the fussing stopped. "How old is he? About three months?"

"Eleven weeks." Her jaw literally dropped. "How did you get him to settle down?"

"He's curious. Is that right, *mijo?* You're figuring out who I am before you start making noise and complaining."

"Let's get him fed before that happens."

She maneuvered in her kitchen with a graceful economy of motion. Her age, he guessed, was probably about thirty—the prime of womanhood, old enough to be done with girlish giggles and young enough to be open to new experience. The more he saw of Emma Richardson, the more he liked her.

After she handed him a bottle full of formula and placed two coffee mugs on the kitchen table, she said, "I made notes of what I remembered about my vision. I'll go get them."

As soon as she left the room, Patrick said, "No rush? I thought you were in a big hurry."

He smiled down at the baby, who smacked his little lips as he sucked down formula. "You didn't tell me she was pretty. How does a woman like that get to be in her late twenties and still unmarried?"

The sheriff sipped his coffee. Wryly, he said, "Maybe because she's a witch, and she turns her lovers into toads."

That was a chance Miguel might be willing to take if it meant spending more time with Emma. He settled Jack into a baby seat on the tabletop and kept the nipple plugged into his mouth. With the other hand, he lifted his coffee mug. The brew was lightly flavored with cinnamon, just the way he liked it.

Emma returned with a sheet of paper, which she placed on the table in front of her. "I'm not quite sure how to interpret everything I saw, but I believe Aspen is alive."

Miguel's infatuation slipped a few notches. Crazy wasn't appealing. "Why?"

"Two reasons. I saw an aspen tree with green leaves.

And the man who was chasing me in the vision said so. He said, 'Aspen got away.' I assume that means he failed to kill my cousin."

"What else?" Patrick asked.

"I was next to a river. For me, water is a symbol of life. The river was to my right, to the east." She frowned at her notes. "Directions seemed to be important, but I'm not sure why. It might have something to do with the medicine wheel."

"The medicine wheel?"

"I'm part Ute. I was raised by my aunt Rose on the rez, and the medicine wheel is part of my culture. The east where the sun rises is associated with good things, new life. I always orient my desk toward the east so my work will go easier. West is the opposite. North is negative. South is positive."

"This vision of yours," Miguel said, trying hard not to be sarcastic. "Was it a road map to find your cousin?"

"I'm not sure what the directions mean. I'm hoping that if I take a look at Aspen's car, I might get a clearer picture of where she is."

"Like a psychic GPS system?"

Anger flashed in her blue eyes. Though Patrick had told him to be nice, Miguel couldn't help teasing. Not when she left herself wide-open with such an irrational theory.

Her tone was curt. "You're a forensic investigator, right?"

"Correct."

"Here's something specific for you to work with." She pushed the paper toward him. "The man who was chasing me wore a leather necklace with a bear claw design. This is what it looked like."

"A grizzly paw." His gaze slid down the page and saw the words in quotation marks: *Aspen got away. But you will die.* Emma hadn't mentioned that second part. Was that the way visions worked? Pick one thing and ignore another?

He also saw another scribbled design using the initials

VDG. That was a symbol he recognized; it was important to another investigation. "What's this?"

"I didn't see it in my vision. When I started making notes, I just drew it."

He adjusted Jack's bottle. "You don't know where it came from? You've never seen it before?"

"Not that I recall."

Her smile was a treasure. So beautiful, *muy bonita*. And so crazy, *muy loca*.

He needed to inform the FBI about the VDG symbol.

## Chapter Two

On their way to the impound lot where Aspen's car was being held, Emma rode with Miguel in her little gas-saving hybrid so they wouldn't have to switch the baby seat in and out of the sheriff's cruiser. Though they were in her car, she let Miguel drive so as not to further affront his authority. His sarcasm clearly told her that he didn't much care for mediums, psychics or spirit visions. The only thing that sparked his interest was that VDG scribble.

She stole a glance at this dark, lean man with the shaggy black hair and dark green eyes—the color of a cool, deep forest. When he wasn't making smart-alecky comments, he was attractive. And she wasn't the only one who thought so. Baby Jack adored him; they'd bonded in seconds. After finishing his bottle, Jack wiggled cheerfully in Miguel's arms and made gurgle noises that sounded like an alien language. Riding in the backseat, Jack still hadn't stopped burbling. His was the only conversation in the car.

Emma couldn't think of a word to say. Though she'd always been terminally shy, this long silence was ridiculous. She cleared her throat. "The snow is melting fast."

"Yeah, it's about time it started feeling like spring," he said.

More silence.

"So, Miguel, are you new to Kenner City?"

"I've been here about a year. I was one of the first employees at the new crime lab."

"Where are you from?"

"You tell me." He shot her a wry glance. "You're the psychic. You're supposed to know these things."

Usually, she paid no attention to those who doubted her visions or—even worse—those who treated her with great deference as if she were the Oracle of Delphi. But she wanted Miguel to accept her. Maybe because he was good with the baby. Maybe because he could help her find Aspen. And maybe…just because. "Are you challenging me?"

"Go ahead. Astound me."

"Fine." She studied him for a moment. His identity shouldn't be so hard to figure out.

The sheriff had mentioned that most of the employees at the lab were from Colorado. She assumed that Miguel wasn't newly transplanted from a big city like Denver; his cowboy boots were well-worn and looked like his habitual footwear. He didn't have the roughened hands of a cowboy or a farmer from the San Luis Valley, but she noticed calluses on his fingertips, typical of a guitar player.

She figured that he'd gone to college to study forensics. But where? Which school? She remembered that when he looked at the design on her pursuer's necklace, he identified the marking as a grizzly claw. Not a bear, but a grizzly. And the grizzly was the school mascot for Adams State College in Alamosa.

"I'm not sure if you were born there," she said, "but you lived in Alamosa."

"Correct." He arched an eyebrow. "The sheriff told you, right? Everybody thinks Patrick Martinez is the strong, silent type, but he can't keep his mouth shut."

"I never heard your name until I met you this morning."

He pulled up at a stop sign, pushed his sunglasses up

on his forehead and stared at her with an intensity that she found both intimidating and sexy. As his gaze scanned her face, searching for a hint that she was lying, she faced him without flinching.

He asked, "What else can you tell me?"

"You play guitar."

He held out his right hand. "You saw the calluses."

"You've got a fresh grease stain on your jeans. Maybe you ride a motorcycle."

"A Harley," he confirmed. "You're using logic. Not psychic intuition."

"Does it matter if I find the answers with logic or by a vision?" she asked earnestly. "Both are methods of observation. Different paths that lead to the same truth. You'd understand if you could be inside my head, walk a mile in my shoes."

He glanced at her feet. "Purple sneakers with white stars? I don't think so."

"They match my jacket." She ran her fingers down the zipper of the purple leather jacket she'd bought on her last trip to New York. The style was so *not* from the Southwest, but she loved it.

As her tone lightened to match his teasing, she realized that she was enjoying this conversation. Moments ago, she'd been tongue-tied. Now her wits were fully engaged. How lovely to talk to an adult who wasn't a nagging ghost. "We have more in common than you think, Miguel. We're both investigators."

"But you see things that aren't visible to the naked eye."

"So do you. Every time you look into a microscope."

"You make a good point." His brow furrowed. "So much of forensics, like DNA testing and trace evidence analysis, isn't readily visible."

"Paranormal phenomenon is the same thing. It exists,

but nobody has invented the tools to accurately reveal these signs and symbols."

Until someone created a reading device, it was up to people like her—psychics and mediums—to interpret.

They parked outside the ten-foot-tall chain-link fence surrounding the police impound lot. The person in charge wasn't a police officer in uniform, but a crusty gray-haired man who looked like he knew his way around a junkyard. As soon as Miguel showed his badge, the old man unlocked the gate and slid it aside.

After a brief discussion, Miguel agreed to hold the baby so she could concentrate, but he refused to wear the color-fully patterned designer baby sling she'd ordered online. Instead, he tucked the baby in the crook of his arm as he answered his cell phone.

Emma picked her way across the gravel lot where most of the snow had melted. Some of these tightly parked cars and trucks looked like they'd been here for years with their tires gone flat and the paint jobs dulled by constant exposure to the elements. Aspen's beat-up sedan seemed new in comparison.

The last time Emma saw this vehicle, shortly after her cousin disappeared, she'd felt confusion and fear as she imagined the desperation Aspen must have experienced as she fled. Similar emotions roiled inside her, but this fear came from her own terrible foreboding that her cousin was never coming back. *Please, Aspen, you have to be alive.* She had so much to live for. Her son. Her new job as a teacher on the rez. After years of struggling and working lousy jobs at the Ute casino and in Las Vegas, Aspen had finally finished college at the University of Nevada. She'd been so close to reaching her dreams.

Miguel strolled up beside her. His calm, no-nonsense attitude reassured her. "That was Patrick on the phone. He has other police business and won't be joining us. When we're done here, can you give me a ride back to the lab?"

"Sure." She circled the hood of the car, hoping to get a clue that would lead to her cousin.

"What are you doing?" he asked.

"Sometimes, when I touch things, I can tap into a spirit energy. In my vision, I saw the car. It must be important."

"If your cousin isn't dead…" He shook his head. "I can't believe I'm saying this."

"Keep going," she encouraged. "A mile in my shoes."

"If your cousin isn't dead, what spirit are you hoping to contact?"

"I saw a woman wearing an FBI jacket. I'm not sure, but I think her name is Julie."

He reacted with a start. "And she's dead?"

"Yes."

His jaw tensed. "Don't play games with me, Emma. You heard something about the FBI investigation. Correct?"

"I haven't heard anything. Why would I?"

"The sheriff mentioned it. Or you heard local gossip."

His accusations irritated her. "I've barely been out of my house for five weeks, ever since Jack came to live with me."

"What about before that?"

"I live alone, and I work at home. When I get together with friends, we don't discuss FBI investigations." She confronted him directly. "Who is Julie?"

"Agent Julie Grainger. She was murdered in January."

She heard the cry of a bird and whirled around. Crows symbolized death for her. When her aunt Rose passed away, a flock of the big black birds had blanketed her yard. Their cries had been deafening.

She looked up, searched the blue skies and saw nothing. No birds at all. But she'd heard something.

There was another chirp, and she realized the sound

came from Jack. Miguel stroked the baby's head. "It's okay, *mijo*. You're a good boy."

"Did you know Julie?"

"A little." His jaw unclenched. "Are you okay, Emma? You look pale."

"As if I've seen a ghost?"

When he smiled, his demeanor changed from hostile to gentle. "I guess that happens a lot to you."

"Too much." She glanced at Jack when he made another chirp. "Maybe you should take the baby back to my car. I don't want to frighten him."

"Are you going to do something scary? Roll around on the ground? Squawk like a chicken? Do a voodoo dance?"

When she glared at him, he grinned.

"You like to tease," she said.

"Life is too sad not to laugh. I mean no disrespect." He rested his hand on her shoulder. His touch was steady and strong as an anchor in a storm. "Do whatever you need to do. I'm here for you. Nothing bad is going to happen."

A dark mist rolled in at the edge of her vision. She'd just told him to go away, but now she wanted him to stay close, wanted to maintain physical contact. "Don't go anywhere."

"You got it."

She laid her palm on the hood of the car. Her sight narrowed. Though still aware of the cars and snow in the impound lot, she seemed to be peering down a tunnel. At the end, she saw the tall woman in an FBI jacket. Julie Grainger. Beside her was a teenage girl in a lovely white gown. Words and images raced through Emma's mind. Rapid-fire. Like film on fast-forward.

Then the vision was gone.

"What is it?" Miguel asked.

Her brain sorted the jumbled impressions. The aspen had been leafy and green. *Her cousin was still alive.* Julie told her Aspen had escaped. Then she'd made a weaving motion with her hand. A river? A snake? "A trail," Emma said. "I should start at the beginning and follow the trail."

"From the crime scene."

"Yes. We should start there." Emma had also seen the VDG symbol again. "VDG is important."

Again, Miguel's interest picked up. "Is VDG connected to your cousin's disappearance?"

"It could be."

She remembered the girl in the white dress. Her presence had nothing to do with Aspen. *She was Miguel's sister. Teresa.* She had died young, less than a year after her *quinceanera,* the ceremony and party that celebrated the fifteenth birthday of a young woman. Teresa wanted her brother to know that she was all right, that she'd found the light and gone to the other side. Teresa believed that Miguel would understand.

But Emma wasn't sure. Though Miguel seemed more open to her ability as a medium, he might not be ready for contact with his tragically dead sister, and she didn't want to alienate him. She needed Miguel to help her find Aspen.

Looking into his eyes, she measured her words, trying to find a balance between proving to him that she wasn't a phony and not freaking him out. Teresa had shown her a family photo with Miguel standing beside his brother, who appeared to be the same age. She said, "You're a twin."

He nodded slowly.

"Fraternal, not identical. Alike, but different."

The silver medal he wore around his neck on a chain glittered in the sunlight. Though she couldn't make out the design, it didn't appear to be a saint. Instinctively, she reached toward it. When her fingers touched the surface, her hand glowed. She identified the image on the front: El Santuario de Chimayo, near Taos in New Mexico.

"Chimayo," she said. A legendary healing place like Lourdes. The words etched on the back of his medal were *Protect and Heal.* Teresa wanted her to know that Miguel had been near death, close enough to see the light.

His near-death experience was why her ability to communicate with dead people threatened him. He knew she was telling the truth, knew there was something beyond this world. He'd been there.

IN THE BACK OF HER CAR, the baby had begun to fuss, and Miguel knew their time for further investigating was limited. He didn't want to believe that Emma's pronouncements were anything more than random guesses, but he couldn't ignore her accuracy. How the hell did she know he was a twin? How had she described his relationship with his brother, Dylan, so accurately? Alike but different. That pretty much summed it up. They were both in law enforcement, but Miguel relied on forensic science while Dylan was a supermacho FBI agent.

Emma reached toward the backseat, hoping to calm Jack. "I should get him back home."

*"Mijo,"* Miguel said. "Give us a break. You'll be okay."

Immediately, Jack's cries modified to quiet little sniffles. He was a good baby, a good boy.

"Amazing," Emma said. "I can't believe the way he responds to your voice. It's almost like you're his father."

"His father is a pig. If *mijo* was my baby boy, I would never abandon him. Family is everything."

"But you're not married."

"Don't remind me." Though he and his brother were thirty-three, neither of the Acevedo twins had found a wife and settled down. "I get enough nagging from my mama."

The leftover snow had melted enough that he could pull onto the shoulder at the edge of the road. This area—where

Aspen's vehicle had been found—was outside Kenner City, but there were houses within sight. There had been no witnesses, no one who stepped forward and said they heard her scream.

"This is it," Emma said. "The start of the trail."

"We won't find anything here. I did the crime scene analysis. There's nothing more to be learned."

Not unless she did that weird vision thing. When she'd touched the car in the impound lot, he'd felt the tension in her body. She seemed to catch her breath. Her blue eyes went blank as a corpse. *Muy loca,* like a trance. But it had lasted less than a minute. If he hadn't been standing beside her with his hand on her shoulder, he wouldn't have noticed.

She shoved her car door open. "I want to take a look around. Jack seems okay. We can leave him in his car seat."

Reluctantly, he joined her. If she managed to somehow turn up evidence that had been overlooked, he needed to be with her to verify and to maintain proper procedure.

Her gaze scanned from left to right and back again. What could she possibly hope to find? The blizzard had erased any footprints. He and the other crime scene investigators had already measured and photographed the skid marks on the pavement.

She lifted her chin and gave a sniff.

"Now what?" he asked. "Are you channeling a bloodhound to scent the trail?"

Instead of bristling, she chuckled. "Might be handy to have a ghost dog. I wouldn't have to pick up the poop."

"You made a joke, Emma."

"But you didn't laugh."

"On the inside, I'm in stitches."

"Seriously," she said, "were search dogs involved?"

"There wasn't time before the blizzard hit." And he regretted that they hadn't been able to call on that resource to locate her cousin. "We only had a few hours to process the scene, and the sheriff's first concern was taking care of Jack."

"I know. As soon as he checked the car's registration, he came to me with the baby." Guilt furrowed her brow. "I should have been here, should have gone out into the snow to look for my cousin. But I was overwhelmed. I wasn't prepared to care for an infant."

"You managed."

"Only because I could order all the baby equipment online. I hired someone to come in four hours a day so I can get my work done, but I'm still sleep-deprived. Sometimes I'm so exhausted that I think I'm losing my mind."

"Losing your mind?" He couldn't resist teasing. "How can you tell?"

"Very funny," she said. "Laughing on the inside."

She walked to the intersection, turned and walked back toward him. Her purple sneakers dug into the snow and mud. Then she went in the opposite direction.

Noises from the baby seat in the back of her SUV reminded him that they didn't have much time. "We can come back here later."

She hunkered down beside a pile of dirty snow. "Over here."

He joined her. The dark leather of the medallion stood out against the snow. The black design, etched into the leather, was a grizzly paw print.

# Chapter Three

The coffee at the Morning Ray Café on the main street of Kenner City wasn't as good as the cinnamon-flavored brew at Emma's house, but Miguel signaled the waitress for a refill as he checked his wristwatch. Dylan was more than fifteen minutes late.

It wasn't like his by-the-book, precise twin to be off schedule by more than a couple of seconds. Ever since Dylan had arrived in Kenner City, he'd been preoccupied; the inside of his head was crammed full with old guilt and new grief. *Numero uno* was the recent murder of Dylan's friend and colleague, Agent Julie Grainger. He and three other FBI agents were working overtime on their investigation of Vincent Del Gardo, the former Las Vegas crime boss suspected of Agent Grainger's murder.

Miguel gave a nod to the cute, red-haired waitress who filled his coffee mug. When she grinned and crinkled her nose, her freckles danced. "How are things at the lab? Solve any big crimes lately?"

"Have you committed any?"

"Not today." She took her order pad from her apron pocket. "What else can I get you?"

"Nothing now, Annie."

She was one of the few people in town he knew by name.

He ate a lot of his meals at this cozy little diner where the burritos were good, and the posole was *primo*. The head cook and owner was Nora Martinez, the sheriff's mother.

Because it was after three o'clock with the lunch rush over and only four other people in the place, Annie lingered at his booth. "Waiting for somebody?"

"My brother."

"The FBI agent." Her smile grew ten times brighter. "He's really cute."

Women had always responded to Dylan as if he were a rock star, which never made sense. They weren't identical twins but resembled each other a lot, and the *chicas* never threw themselves at Miguel. "Better not let Dylan hear you call him cute. That's a word for baby ducks and puppies."

Annie laughed. "Handsome is a much better word."

If anyone had heard about the FBI investigation, it would be Annie or the people in the café, which was frequented by many of the local law enforcement people. "How much do you know about Dylan's investigation?"

"An agent got murdered. A woman agent. One of the other FBI guys was showing her picture around, asking if we'd seen her or noticed her talking to anyone."

"Thanks, Annie."

Miguel thought Emma might have picked up Agent Julie Grainger's name from talking to someone at the café or someone else who had seen the photograph. That'd be a logical explanation for how she came up with Julie's name. But it didn't explain the VDG symbol or the grizzly paw necklace.

Later this afternoon, he and other forensic technicians would process the necklace in the hope that they might discover the identity of the owner. They probably wouldn't be lucky enough to find fingerprints—not after it had been buried in the snow at the side of the road all this time.

How the hell had he missed finding the necklace when they first swept the scene? Sure, the leather was the color of dirt and would have blended in when there wasn't snow on the ground. Sure, they'd had other urgent tasks—dusting for prints, measuring skid marks, photographing footprints. Sure, there was a blizzard on the way. But he wouldn't easily forgive himself for overlooking such an obvious clue.

He had to be shown the way by a medium. By Emma. *La loca bonita.* A crazy, beautiful lady in a purple leather jacket.

Dylan came through the front door of the café and joined him in the corner booth. "Sorry I'm late."

"No *problemo.* You okay?"

"Don't worry about me, *vato.*"

Dylan had always been the tough guy, the star athlete, the macho leader of the pack. It bothered Miguel to see his brother rattled.

Annie rushed to their booth as soon as Dylan sat down. She placed a steaming mug of coffee in front of his brother and set down two pieces of apple pie.

"On the house," she said in a throaty voice. She leaned close to Dylan, giving him a glimpse of cleavage. "Is there anything else you want?"

Miguel couldn't resist this setup. "My brother likes whipped cream. All over his pie."

Dylan raised a hand. "Not necessary."

The waitress fluttered her lashes. "You can have all the whipped cream you want. Your name is Dylan, right? And I'm Annie."

*And I'm yesterday's fish stew.* Amused, Miguel leaned back in the booth and watched as his brother doled out the charm. The guy couldn't help it. He was a *chica* magnet.

When Annie finally moved away, Dylan said, "What's so important that I had to see you right away?"

"The sheriff and I met with a woman today. Her name is Emma Richardson."

Annie rushed back to their booth. "I love Emma," she gushed. "She's a real psychic, you know. She sees things. And she finds missing people."

"Thanks for your opinion," Miguel said in a quiet, firm tone of dismissal. The time for fun and games was over. He needed to talk seriously with his brother. "We'll call you if we need anything else."

"Enjoy your pie." She turned on her heel and flounced back toward the counter.

"A psychic," Dylan grumbled as he dug into his pie. "You interrupted my day to talk about a psychic."

"I was skeptical, too." Miguel kept his voice low so Annie wouldn't come running back over to them. "You know I don't like things that can't be explained by logic or science."

"You were always the smart brother. *El Ganso.*" He smirked. *"El Nerdo Supremo."*

"Because I think with my head, not my *huevos.*" Miguel fixed his twin with a cool gaze. This wasn't a time for joking. "I took the psychic—actually, she's a medium— back to the crime scene where Aspen Meadows disappeared. She had a vision that turned up an important piece of evidence."

Though Dylan continued to eat his pie, Miguel sensed that his brother was interested. "The sheriff still doesn't have any leads on the missing woman?"

"Not yet. I don't have much hope. Somebody who's missing for over a month is either dead or doesn't want to be found." He frowned. "But Emma Richardson is certain that Aspen is alive. They're cousins, and Emma is the guardian for the baby."

"The father hasn't come forward?"

"Not yet." Miguel took out the piece of paper Emma had used to make her notes from the vision. He spread it on the table in front of his brother. "She drew the design of the leather necklace we found at the scene. And also, she drew this."

Dylan picked up paper. His eyes narrowed. "VDG. Vincent Del Gardo."

"There was a symbol like this on that map you showed me—the map that Agent Grainger sent before she died."

Miguel and everybody else in the crime lab had tried every way possible to decipher that map. From satellite GPS to old-fashioned cartography, no one could make sense of those weird twists and turns. It didn't match any known roads. The map could have been the path of a spreading river. Or trails through the forest.

At the counter, Annie was joking and laughing too loudly with a guy who had been sitting there since Miguel came in. He overheard the word *psychic* and glanced toward them. They had to be talking about Emma, and that bothered him. He checked out the guy so he'd remember what he looked like. He wouldn't be easy to forget. Though big and barrel-chested, he was a sharp dresser in a fringed leather jacket with a turquoise yoke. The band around his cowboy hat was snakeskin with the rattles still attached.

Dylan tapped nervously on the tabletop. His voice went low and quiet. "What does this part of the note mean? A tall woman in an FBI jacket."

There was no easy way to say this. "Emma's spirit guide for this vision was Julie."

"She saw Julie?"

"In the same sense that she sees everything. In her head."

"If this is true," Dylan said, "it means that the missing woman is connected to Vincent Del Gardo. Connected to Julie's murder."

"*Sí*, I know."

"This is big. It opens a whole new line of investigation."

"Are you still searching for Del Gardo?"

Dylan nodded. "And for the money he's got stashed away."

Miguel had heard that Del Gardo's illegal fortune was in excess of fifty million dollars. Not an amount that could be tucked away in a tidy little suitcase. "Your map with the VDG symbol might lead to both."

"Let's see if your psychic can point us in the right direction."

BEFORE BABY JACK showed up on her doorstep, the bathroom in Emma's house had been tidy with feminine decorative touches. Now, she had no time for long baths, scented candles and fresh flowers. Her mosaic-tiled countertop held a variety of baby products. She'd known that her life would be different if a man moved in, but she hadn't expected pacifiers and butt wipes.

Confronting her reflection in the mirror, she dabbed a glob of spit-up off the shoulder of her beige turtleneck and ran a comb through her chin-length brown hair. Miguel had called and asked if he and his FBI brother could stop by and ask a few questions.

*Miguel.* She sighed. *Miguel Acevedo.* She wouldn't mind having him as a houseguest. He was definitely handsome with those green eyes and strong features, but his greater appeal came from his quick mind. She had to be alert when she was around him. He was a challenge.

Also, she needed him to find Aspen. *To follow the trail.* But where was this trail? Discovering the necklace in the snow was a start, but Emma had no idea what came next.

In the mirror, standing beside her, was Grandma Quinn. The resemblance between her and this blue-eyed, elderly lady made her smile.

Grandma said, "Why don't you change that shirt, dear?"

Emma didn't need fashion tips from the other side. "You know I had a vision about Aspen."

"About time."

"I'm supposed to follow a trail or a path. Do you know anything about that?"

"Change the shirt."

Grandma faded and vanished, leaving Emma frustrated. All too often, her spirit visits were cryptic hints and vague impressions instead of direct instructions. Why couldn't Grandma Quinn give her a street address or a phone number?

Grabbing the baby monitor, she hurried to the front door and onto the porch to wait for Miguel and his brother. Jack had finally fallen asleep, and she didn't want the baby wakened by two grown men tromping through the house.

When the car pulled into her driveway, a shiver of anticipation went through her, making her realize how glad she was to be seeing Miguel again. He gave her a lopsided grin that made her heart beat a little faster.

His twin brother resembled him, but she would never confuse these two men. There was something about Miguel that drew her closer. His was a healing presence, like the words inscribed on the back of his silver Chimayo medal.

As she shook hands with Dylan—whose handsome face was somehow enhanced by the scar on his chin—she had the impression that he was kind of scary. His eyes looked haunted. Not in the sense that he had ghosts hanging around him, but he had secrets, many secrets. And he had seen terrible things.

"I hope you two don't mind," she said, "but I'd rather stay outside. The baby's asleep, and I don't want to wake him."

She directed them to a flagstone path that led to the covered patio behind her house. The afternoon sun warmed this western exposure, and there were only a few patches of snow left behind from the blizzard. Within the month, she hoped to start planting her vegetable garden. Most of her other landscaping was shrubs and annual flowers, indigenous to the high plains so they didn't need much watering in drought years.

She sat at the round wrought-iron table with one twin on either side. Miguel held the piece of paper upon which she'd written her impressions from her first vision this morning. "We wanted to talk about the VDG symbol," he said.

*With the* V *standing for Virgin?* She sucked in a breath to keep from blurting an embarrassing comment. "I really don't know where that came from."

"How does that work?" Miguel asked.

"It's called automatic writing," she said. "Another way the dead communicate through me. I'm holding the pen, but they are directing the strokes. Some people call it channeling."

Watching her intently, he asked, "Does the name Vincent Del Gardo mean anything to you?"

She probed her memory and shrugged. "Nothing comes to mind."

"He's from Las Vegas."

"I've only been there twice." The memory made her smile. "I went to visit Aspen while she was going to college there. She thought, because I'm a medium, that I might be able to beat the odds at gambling. We tried roulette, craps and blackjack. I was lousy at all of them."

Dylan leaned forward. "Your cousin might have mentioned Del Gardo. He had interests in several casinos. Maybe she worked for him."

"I don't recall." In her mind, she repeated the name. *Vincent Del Gardo.* "Are you looking for him? Is he missing?"

"Maybe you can find him," Miguel said. "When you do

that missing persons thing with the sheriff, what's the process?"

"Everything I see or hear in a vision comes from someone on the other side. When I'm asleep, they come to me as if in a dream. When I touch something connected with a missing person, I sometimes intersect with the psychic energy of someone close to them who has passed away. I see them. And hear them."

"Give me specifics," Miguel said. "Last fall, when you told the sheriff that the missing boy was with his father in a motel in Durango, how did you do it?"

"I touched some of the boy's clothing. My vision came from his dead grandmother. She showed me a vision of the room, a wagon wheel and the number seven."

"You're a medium," Dylan said. "The FBI works with mediums. I get it."

Miguel asked, "Were you always like this?"

"When I was ten years old, Grandma Quinn appeared to me. I was old enough to know that my grandmother was dead and to understand what that meant."

"What did she look like?" Miguel asked.

"Just the way she looked in life. But not solid. The best comparison I can make is a hologram. Grandma Quinn wasn't scary, she hadn't come to frighten me. She gave me a warning. It saved my life."

Grandma Quinn had told her there was danger, told her that Emma and her mother had to leave the house. Though ten-year-old Emma wept and pleaded, her mother wouldn't listen.

Later that night, when her mother's abusive boyfriend came home, Emma fled. She ran next door to the neighbor's and hammered on the door. Remembering caused her hands to draw into fists. Sobbing, Emma had begged them to call the police.

They arrived too late. There was a fire in her mother's bedroom. Both she and her boyfriend were killed.

"Emma," Miguel said, "what are you thinking about?"

"A memory." She met his gaze and saw his struggle to accept what she was saying. "A real-life memory. I'm not crazy."

"We get it," Dylan said loudly, demanding her attention. "You knew the missing woman. Aspen Meadows."

"I grew up with her. After my mother died, I went to live with my aunt Rose on the rez." She gestured to her brown hair and blue eyes. "I didn't fit in with the other kids. Aspen used to tease me, and she resented that I was taking Aunt Rose's attention away from her. My main goal in life was to get off the reservation. I studied hard and got a full scholarship to University of Colorado when I was sixteen."

"You sound like my brother," Dylan said.

*"El Nerdo Supremo,"* Miguel said.

"Perfect description." She laughed on the inside. "Anyway, Aspen and I got along better as adults. I kept pushing her to go to college, and she had finally finished her studies. She was coming back to the rez to be a teacher."

A cry from the baby monitor alerted her. "Excuse me? It's almost time for Jack's feeding. I need to get a bottle of formula ready."

She hurried into the house through the back door. Still listening to the baby monitor, she went through the motions of preparing the bottle and measuring the formula. *Vincent Del Gardo.* A casino owner from Las Vegas.

She glanced through the kitchen window. Beyond the patio where the twin brothers sat in conversation, she saw a third person—a man with a shaved head and a white beard. A ghost.

When he looked toward her and waved, she saw his black-framed glasses. He returned to his task, digging with a spade in the area where she would soon plant her garden. The hole grew quickly. He reached inside and pulled out a handful of gold coins.

She blinked, and he was gone.

The noises from the baby monitor grew more insistent, but she rushed outside to the patio table. "Buried treasure. Does Del Gardo have something to do with treasure?"

Dylan stood. "What did you see?"

"An old man with a shaved head and white beard. Thick glasses. He dug up a handful of gold coins."

"That description doesn't fit Del Gardo," Dylan said. "To the best of our knowledge, he's not dead."

"Maybe it wasn't him. The man I saw didn't seem like a crime boss. He was kindly. Like a favorite uncle."

"Do you know his name?" Dylan asked.

"No." If she'd known something as obvious as a name, Emma would have mentioned it. She didn't much care for Dylan's attitude. Though he'd been quick to accept her abilities as a medium, he seemed hostile.

"I want to show you the other VDG symbol," he said. "After I return to headquarters to pick up that evidence, I'll be back with my other colleagues."

"Not tonight," she said.

"What?" His tone was abrupt. Apparently, Dylan wasn't accustomed to having his decisions questioned. "Why not?"

"If this symbol leads to other evidence, I need to be free to follow the trail."

"The trail?" Dylan glanced toward his brother.

Miguel explained, "A trail of evidence that might lead to Emma's cousin."

"Tonight," she said, "I need to stay with the baby. Tomorrow morning, I have someone who comes in to watch him."

"Tomorrow morning, nine o'clock," Dylan said, turning

on his heel and stalking along the flagstone path toward the front of the house. "Let's go, Miguel."

He rose slowly. His gaze focused on the formula bottle in her hand. "If you want, I can stay. I can help with *mijo*."

Though it would be wonderful to have his help, she shook her head. "It's better for me if you go with your brother and calm him down. I don't want him to come back tomorrow with a dozen federal agents. I can't let this turn into a sideshow."

He gently took her free hand. "Dylan plows straight ahead like a powerboat and throws up a big wake. You need a more quiet approach. Like a silent canoe across the waters."

She smiled, appreciating his imagery. A silent canoe.

It had taken five long weeks for her to get any hint about Aspen's disappearance, and she didn't want to jeopardize this tenuous connection with a huge fanfare and many curious eyes watching her. "I want you to come back tomorrow with your brother. Only you."

He gave her hand a squeeze, and she felt a pleasant ripple chase up her arm.

"Tomorrow," he said. "You have my cell-phone number. Call me if you need anything."

She watched as he sauntered along the flagstone path, and she was tempted to call him back. Miguel made her feel safe and protected. She wanted him to stay close to her.

But there wasn't time right now to indulge in such a fantasy. She returned to the house and went directly to her bedroom where Jack's bassinette sat beside her four-poster bed. His little face scrunched up as he let out a loud cry.

"It's okay," she said. "It's okay, *mijo*." Miguel's word for the baby slipped easily through her lips. She liked the way it sounded.

As she lifted him onto her shoulder, she heard the front

doorbell. Was it Miguel coming back? She rushed through the house and opened the door.

Standing on her front stoop was a very large man in a fringed leather jacket with a turquoise yoke.

## Chapter Four

Only a flimsy, unlocked screen door stood between Emma and this stranger. In spite of his colorful jacket, he was dark and dangerous. She didn't need a psychic vision to know that she'd be crazy to invite this man into her house.

He must have noticed her hesitation because he stepped back a pace and politely removed his brown cowboy hat. The band was snakeskin with the rattles still attached. His thinning hair, streaked with gray, lay flat against his skull. His attempt at a smile seemed like an aberration, as if his face were unaccustomed to friendly expressions.

"My name is Hank Bridger," he said in a whispery voice. "Are you Emma Richardson?"

"Yes." Still holding Jack on her shoulder, she calculated how long it would take for her to slam the door and race through the house to safety. She had a pistol on the upper shelf in her bedroom closet, but it wasn't loaded.

"Annie at the Morning Ray Café told me that you're a psychic. She gave me your address."

*Thanks a heap, Annie.* "What else did she tell you?"

"That you can help me." The attempted smile slipped off his long face. Deep lines carved furrows across his forehead and around his mouth. "Ma'am, I'd be willing to pay for your time."

"I'm sorry, Mr. Bridger. Annie gave you the wrong impression. I'm not for hire."

"I'm trying to find my brother. He's been missing since January, and I'm at the end of my rope."

She couldn't help being sympathetic to Bridger's cause. Like her, he was searching for a relative who had disappeared.

Jack wriggled on her shoulder and she lowered him to the crook of her arm. He waved his little arms and let out a yell. "The baby is due for a feeding. This isn't a convenient time."

"I can come back." He slapped his hat back onto his head. "Later tonight?"

"Not tonight," she said firmly. "But maybe tomorrow afternoon. I can't promise that I'll be able to help you."

"How does it work when you get these visions? Annie said you have to touch something that belonged to the missing person."

"Sometimes that helps. If you'll excuse me, I—"

Without warning, he whipped open the screen door, grasped her hand and pressed a round disc into her palm. He stepped back immediately, allowing the door to swing shut.

The suddenness shocked her. Who would have thought such a big man could move so fast? Looking down at her hand, she saw a hundred-dollar poker chip.

"Las Vegas," she said. That explained a lot. Bridger was a Vegas cowboy, not someone who actually rode the range.

"Vegas is my brother's hometown."

Was Hank Bridger somehow connected with Vincent Del Gardo, the casino owner? Though it seemed an unlikely coincidence, she firmly believed that everything happened for a reason. Bridger might lead to the next step on the path to finding her cousin.

She turned the chip over in her hand. The outer circle

of dark gold was edged with green letters spelling out Centurion Casino. She'd been to that Roman-themed establishment when she visited Aspen. She remembered lots of marble and elephant statues.

Bridger leaned closer to the screen door. "You see something. What can you tell me?"

Jack gave a series of yips—sounds that usually led to sustained wailing. And she couldn't blame him. He was hungry. "I have to go."

"Keep the chip," he said. "I'll be back tomorrow afternoon."

As he walked down the sidewalk, she closed the front door and flipped the dead bolt. Though it was possible that destiny had brought Hank Bridger to her doorstep, the fates weren't always kind. In her early morning vision, the man with the leather necklace wanted to kill her. Bridger—in his fringed jacket and snakeskin boots—wasn't that man. But there might be a connection. She needed to be cautious.

While she got Jack changed, she considered taking her gun down from the top shelf and loading it. Probably not a good plan. She hadn't fired the gun in over three years.

Leaning over the changing table, she nuzzled Jack's tummy. "I'd probably shoot my foot off."

He giggled in response.

"Yes, indeedy." She crooned as she picked up his tiny pink feet and kissed his toes. "Yes, I would. I'd probably shoot my footsie right off."

Having a baby in the house changed everything. If Emma had been alone, she wouldn't have been so concerned about Bridger. But there was more than her own safety to worry about. She might need help. It occurred to her that Miguel was only a phone call away.

With Jack freshly diapered and dressed in a green-and-yellow footed sleeper, she settled with him in the solidly built, antique rocking chair with the carved oak back. Before the baby came to live with her, she hardly ever used this piece of furniture. But the rocking chair made a perfect nest for bottle feeding. As soon as she plugged the nipple in his mouth, he slurped vigorously.

Her gaze surveyed her eclectic living room. From the clean lines of the beige patterned sofa to the burgundy velvet Queen Anne chair, she'd picked every piece with care, sparing no expense. She focused on the telephone resting on the spindle-legged table. Would Miguel think she was too needy if she called? Or was she being prudent and sensible? Hank Bridger was a menacing character who had come out of nowhere.

After Jack was fed, she paced with the baby on her shoulder. More than an hour had passed since Bridger came to her door. If he intended to return, he would have done so. Unless he was waiting for darkness.

*Better safe than sorry.* She picked up the phone and punched in the number on the card Miguel had left behind. He answered after the first ring. "Emma. What's wrong?"

As soon as she heard his voice, she felt like a coward. "I'm probably overreacting. But this guy showed up at my house, wanting me to help him find his missing brother. And he gave me a hundred-dollar chip from the Centurion Casino."

"I'll be right there."

"That's not necessary. I was just wondering if…"

He'd already hung up. As she disconnected, she felt herself smiling. For most of her life, she'd been on her own—proudly independent and able to take care of herself. This was a change. It felt good to have someone to call— a strong, capable man with intoxicating green eyes. A man who could watch over her and *mijo* Jack.

Standing at the front window, she watched through the Irish lace curtains as the sunlight segued into dusk. The house across the street had turned on their lights, probably getting ready to sit down to dinner. Should she offer Miguel something to eat? Like what? She hadn't taken anything out of the freezer this morning to thaw. Her plans for this evening were opening a can of soup or zapping a frozen dinner in the microwave.

His motorcycle thrummed as he swooped up her driveway and parked the sleek, powerful Harley. He wasn't wearing protective headgear. Not illegal, Colorado didn't have helmet laws, but she disapproved of the risk. At the same time, she loved the way his black hair was tousled by the wind. Still astride the Harley, he peeled off his dark glasses and stowed them in the pocket of his denim jacket.

Only once in her life had Emma dared to ride on the back. She'd been terrified. And exhilarated.

She scurried to the front door, flipped the dead bolt and opened it wide. Though the fading sunlight was dim, his green eyes glowed with reassuring warmth.

"I'm glad you called," he said. "I saw what you wrote on that piece of paper where you described your vision."

She'd scribbled a lot of things. "What was that?"

"You made a note. 'Aspen got away, but you will die.'" He stepped inside and looked around, peering into the shadows in the corners. "What made you write that?"

She remembered the faceless man with the knife, the darkness, the blade slashing toward her throat. Some of the things she saw weren't meant to be shared. "You can't take my visions literally. Sometimes, death doesn't necessarily mean physically dying. It could be a death of hope. Or well-being. Or a relationship."

"But I'm a literal kind of guy. You said that you were being chased. Then what?"

"The man with the leather necklace caught me. He had a knife. He said those words."

"The man who came to your door, was it him?"

"I don't think so. He's not the sort of guy who'd wear a beat-up leather necklace. His name is Hank Bridger. He's tall and broad-shouldered. Kind of a snazzy dresser."

"Fringed jacket? A hat with a rattlesnake band?"

She gave a surprised nod. "Now who's the psychic?"

"I saw him in the Morning Ray Café, talking to the waitress." He lifted Jack from her shoulder and nuzzled the top of the baby's head. "Hey, *mijo*, did you miss me?"

Jack gurgled and rewarded him with a great, big smile. He was so sweet, so perfect and innocent. If anything happened to him, she'd never forgive herself. "Bridger claimed to be searching for his brother. He gave me something that belonged to the missing man. A hundred-dollar chip from the Centurion Casino."

"Del Gardo has financial interests in the Centurion."

"I didn't get any particular vibe from the chip."

"No *problemo*. I can."

"Get vibes? How?"

"Fingerprints." He tucked Jack into the crook of his arm. "Show me the way to your computer. Let's do some quick research on Hank Bridger."

She walked through the living room, turning on lights as she went. At the end of the hallway, she opened the door to her office. Very few people had been inside this room. Not the woman who came in twice a month to clean. Not the sitter who took care of Jack in the mornings.

Emma had several reasons to keep her work private. If anyone found out what she was really doing at her computer, her financial well-being would be threatened. This secret couldn't be shared with anyone. Not even Miguel.

As HE WENT THROUGH her house, Miguel switched his brain to analytical mode, as if studying a crime scene. His work

included more than collecting trace evidence. The greater
clues often came from objects or decoration or color. He
could learn much about Emma by studying her home. His
first impression: feminine.

Even if he had spent way too much time noticing her
slender waist and the way her hips flared into a sexy curve,
he would have known a woman lived in this house because
of the velvet chair, the lampshade with dangling red crystals
and the pastel watercolor paintings on the walls. The paintings were signed, maybe originals. Many of the other items
looked expensive. He concluded that Emma was a woman
of varied tastes and had the money to indulge them.

Her office was different. Apart from the high-tech
equipment, it was as plain as a monk's cell. No plants. No
candles. No photos. Papers were stacked and sorted in
bins. One wall, floor to ceiling, was solid books. In an
alcove that had probably once been a closet, he saw file
cabinets and shelving filled with supplies. Two long desks
angled to form an L-shape. One side was a workstation
with her desktop computer, scattered notes and books. The
other held a printer, scanner, fax and copy machine.

Her office was designed for real-life, practical business—nothing psychic or weird. Nothing personal.

"Nice setup," he commented. "What kind of work do
you do?"

"This and that."

An evasive answer if he'd ever heard one. "The sheriff
said you were a consultant."

"That sounds about right."

Most people liked to talk about their area of expertise,
but her lips pressed together as if holding back. Finding out
what she did in this office was the key to understanding a
different side to Emma.

He checked out the titles on the reference books. *How*

*to Build a Bomb. Encyclopedia of Firearms. Deciphering Codes.*

"If I had to guess," he said, "I'd say you were doing consulting work for the Department of Defense."

"Why on earth would you think that?"

"Your reading material looks like you're planning to take over the world. Or training to be a spy." The idea of Emma— a woman who wore purple leather—taking on the world of espionage tickled him. "Or maybe you want to be *macho.*"

"I'll leave that to you," she said as she swept her notes off the desktop and dumped them in the top drawer, which she closed tightly. "Why do you need my computer?"

He passed the baby to her and took a seat in front of the flat screen and keyboard. "I'll link with my computer at the lab, using my password. We'll see if your Hank Bridger has a criminal record."

Computers weren't his specialty, but Miguel knew the basics. Hooking up with the lab computer while he was in the field at a crime scene came in handy. He went through the steps, feeding in Bridger's name—Hank or Henry—for a nationwide search.

"Running this data could take a few minutes."

He stood and cleared his throat to cover the growling from his empty belly. The last thing he'd eaten was the apple pie at the café. When Emma called, he'd been in the parking lot of the Morning Ray, close enough to smell the rich, hot, spicy chili.

Food would have to wait. First, he needed to make sure Emma and *mijo* would be safe for the night. "Do you have a security system on your house? Burglar alarms?"

"Most of the time, I don't even lock the doors. Until recently, Kenner City hasn't been a hotbed of criminal activity." Parallel worry lines appeared between her eyebrows. "Can I offer you dinner?"

*Mucho gusto.* His stomach danced for joy. "I could eat."

"Let's go to the kitchen, and I'll see what I can scare up."

He followed her, catching a glimpse through the open door of her bedroom. The wood on the four-poster bed matched the dresser and side tables. More high-quality stuff. Even Jack's bassinette and changing table were classy. Since he knew she hadn't inherited money, he assumed that whatever kind of work she did in her office paid her very well.

She settled Jack into a baby seat on her kitchen table and flipped the switch on the CD player resting on the countertop. Soft music spilled into the room.

"Classical," he said.

"Not my favorite, but I read somewhere that Mozart is recommended for babies."

Not for any of the babies he knew, but Miguel didn't argue. While she dug through her refrigerator, he surveyed the room from a safety standpoint. The back door seemed solid but didn't have a dead bolt. The three windows looked like they'd been replaced recently and were double-pane. Not that the extra thickness would stop an intruder. If Hank Bridger wanted to get to Emma, those windows wouldn't be an obstacle.

"Do you ever worry about getting robbed?" he asked.

"Not so much. If I'm out of town, I pay someone to house-sit."

The only way for Miguel to guarantee she'd be safe would be to stay here himself. The sheriff didn't have the manpower to provide a bodyguard, and the same was true for the FBI. Law enforcement didn't get involved in protective custody until after an attack. Then, it was too late.

She pulled a container from the freezer. "Lasagna?"

He was starving, and it would take hours to thaw that brick of pasta. "I have a better idea. I'll make a run to the café and pick up a couple of burritos."

"Great idea. Cooking isn't really my thing."

After she shoved the lasagna back into the freezer, she whirled around and beamed an unexpected smile in his direction. The worry in her face disappeared. Her blue eyes shimmered like sunlight on a mountain lake.

The analytical side of his brain shut down. As he stared at her, he forgot the potential danger that brought him here. The soft piano sonata from the CD player painted the air with soft pastels, like her watercolor paintings—colors that suited a gentle, graceful woman with silky brown hair. He almost felt like they were on a date.

"Thank you for coming over here so quickly," she said.

"My pleasure." Earlier he'd been thinking he should stay at her house as a bodyguard. Now he had another reason altogether. He *wanted* to be here, *wanted* to be with her. "I should get going. To the café."

Shyly, she bit her lower lip. "Hurry back."

EMMA WATCHED THROUGH the front window as Miguel climbed onto his Harley and drove away. Calling him had been one of the best decisions she'd ever made.

Humming along to Mozart, she meandered into the kitchen, where she sorted through a few things she could cook for tomorrow. Cooking for Miguel? The thought was both exciting and terrifying. Her culinary talents had never progressed beyond making a salad. Preparing an elaborate dinner for one didn't interest her.

After a little tidying up, she went into her bedroom, placed Jack on the comforter and stretched out beside him. Since her reading time was limited to short spurts between baby care, magazines had taken the place of books. The glossy pages flipped through her fingers and landed on an article titled, "How To Make Him Hot For You."

She scanned the checklist: perfume, lip gloss, smoky

eyes, flirty clothes. Touch him frequently. Find out what you have in common. "Not much," she said to Jack. "We're pretty much opposites."

And she was far too mature to follow the advice of a magazine article. "But maybe a dab of perfume wouldn't hurt."

When she rose from the bed, she saw Grandma Quinn standing in the doorway. Her voice was a thin whisper. "Emma, get out of the house. There's danger."

"What?"

"Take the baby and run."

## Chapter Five

Fear chased Emma backward in time—all the way back to when she was a child. Grandma Quinn had warned her of danger, told her to run away and save herself. In a way, she'd been running ever since. She'd spent her life avoiding risk, keeping safe.

"Why?" she asked the ghostly figure. "What's the danger?"

The pale lips of her grandma formed one word. "Run."

The sound raced around the room, bouncing off walls and ceiling, picking up volume and velocity. *Run, run, run, run, run.* It echoed like rolling thunder.

Grandma Quinn vanished.

Emma's course was clear. She gathered Jack into her arms, grabbed a blanket from the bassinette and shoved her feet into shoes. No time for anything else. Get away from here. Get away fast.

Halfway to the front door, she halted. This was her home, a place she'd lived for years and literally put down roots in the garden. Fear couldn't drive her away. She wasn't a helpless ten-year-old girl with no other option than running to the neighbor's house and beating her fists raw against their closed door.

She called the sheriff's private number. "Patrick, this is Emma. I think somebody's trying to break into my house."

"I'm on it."

And Miguel was on his way back to her house. She and Jack would be all right…unless danger hit before help arrived.

Her gun was tucked away in the closet. If she got it down and loaded, she could defend herself. With a baby in her arms? No way, that was impossibly dangerous.

What should she do? The frightened child that lived inside her wanted to run. The more reasonable adult countered with logic. If Bridger lay in wait outside the door, he'd easily overtake her before she made it across the yard to her neighbors. It was smarter to stay here, to wait for help to arrive. But if she waited too long…

As if sensing her internal struggle, Jack let out a wail.

She hugged him close. "Don't worry. I won't let anything happen to you."

In spite of the confusion and fear that clenched every nerve in her body, a plan formed in her mind. Her car was parked in the driveway right outside. If she could get to the car with Jack, she'd make a clean escape.

She raced into the kitchen and got her car keys from her purse. Go out the back door? Or the front?

Under her breath, she whispered, "Hurry, Miguel."

The wall clock slowly ticked off the seconds. He'd be here soon. He'd protect her and the baby.

As she bounced Jack to calm him, her gaze fixed on the back-door knob. It jiggled, started to turn.

She dashed through the house to the front door and flung it open. Crossing the yard in a few frantic strides, she ripped open the car door and dove behind the steering wheel. She slammed the door, locked it. Turning, she settled Jack into his car seat.

She'd made it. With trembling fingers, she plugged the

key into the ignition. She turned the key and heard a click-ing noise. The engine didn't catch. "No, this can't be hap-pening."

Her foot pumped the gas. Again, she tried to start the car. *Click, click, click.*

Her clever plan had left her trapped. In the moonlight, she saw a figure. A broad-shouldered man. Huge. Dangerous.

Stepping out of the shadows, he approached her car. His face was obscured by the flat brim of his hat.

Her hand rested on the door latch. Should she throw open the door and run? No, she couldn't leave Jack here alone.

The man came closer. Why was he after her? What did he want?

The rumble of a motorcycle cut through the night. It was the sweetest growl she'd ever heard. Miguel was here.

As his headlight flashed in her rear window, she watched the man who had been coming toward her turn away. He slid back into the shadows.

Emma leaped from her car and ran toward Miguel. Toward safety.

EYEBALLING THE BAGS OF FOOD he'd brought from the café, Miguel leaned back in his chair at the end of her kitchen table. Emma sat to his right. On the table beside her was the bouncy baby seat where Jack wiggled and added a running commentary of giggles and goos.

His conversation with the lady of the house hadn't been so cheerful. Moments after she threw herself into his arms, the sheriff had arrived with sirens blaring. Her concern about possible danger had turned into a tangible threat. The lock on her back door—a pathetically simple device—had been picked. The battery cable in her car had been de-tached, which was why she couldn't get a spark. Her at-tacker had meant to trap her with no means of escape.

Miguel tamped down his anger. It served no purpose for him to rage against this faceless coward. Better to move on and hope that their luck got better. Unfortunately, the coward had left no evidence.

The sheriff and his deputies spread out and canvassed the area. They found no witnesses. Though Miguel had dusted, he found no fingerprints. There were no footprints on the flagstone path leading around to the back of her house.

"Who was he?" Emma asked for the hundredth time. "You know more than you're telling."

"*Dios mio,* Emma. Let it go."

"I have a right to know who's after me. And why."

He felt guilty, blamed himself for exposing her to danger. The time for casual protection was over. The sheriff had promised frequent drive-bys throughout the night, and Miguel would stay with her as a bodyguard. His hand instinctively went to his gun holster. "I don't want to drag you deeper into the investigation. I've already told you too much."

"Miguel, please. I've spent most of my life running away, and I'm tired of hiding. More information can't hurt me." She straightened her shoulder. "And I might be able to help."

Solving crimes through her visions was a poor substitute for logic and forensics. But she had a point about information. If she knew what she was up against, it gave her an advantage. "I don't know all the answers."

"Tell me what you can." She rose from the table and took down two plates from the cabinet above the dishwasher. "While you're talking, we can eat."

He tore open the bags. Burritos, churros and posole. It was a feast.

She set a bottled water in front of him and picked at her own food. "Let's start with the easy part. Why would anyone come after me?"

He dodged the question. "Any man with eyes would come after a beauty like you."

"Oh, please. I'm an old maid. Thirty years old and not married."

"*Dios mio!* Thirty years old! You're an ancient crone."

In spite of herself, she grinned. "You're older than I am."

"Thirty-three. A decrepit, old bachelor." He bit into his burrito. "And proud to be unmarried."

"Really? No regrets?"

"Not on my part. But Mama says I owe her grandbabies."

On cue, Jack made a noise that was somewhere between the rat-a-tat of a machine gun and the bleating of a goat. His message was clear: pay attention to me. And Emma did. She reached toward him and tickled his tiny foot.

When she looked at baby Jack, her blue eyes filled with love. "Until this little guy got here, I never thought of myself as someone who would have children. I've always been kind of a loner."

"Except for pop-in visits from ghosts."

He was glad to see her hostile glare. When she had first run to his arms, she'd been devastated by terror. Anger was a much healthier response.

"You've gotten off the subject," she said. "Why is someone coming after me?"

"Are you sure it wasn't Bridger?"

Using her fork, she drew a circle around her head. "The man who came out of the shadows had a hat with a flat brim. Not like Bridger."

He shoveled down another forkful of food. His grateful belly had ceased growling. "I don't have solid evidence to prove why someone would attack you."

"I'll settle for assumptions."

"I have two," he said. "No, make that three."

"Just tell me," she snapped.

"*Numero uno.* Your cousin disappeared, and we still don't know why. She might have information that threatens the bad guys. Something she told you." He took a swig of water. "Did she mention any secrets?"

Emma shook her head, sending a shimmer through her straight, brown hair. "Nothing I can recall."

"We move to my second theory." He hadn't put these thoughts into words until this moment, but the logic fell easily into place. "You keep saying that Aspen is still alive."

"That's right."

"Whoever made her disappear the first time might want to make sure that she never comes back. Maybe he thinks you know where she's hiding."

Emma rose from her chair. "That makes sense. Since I have custody of Jack, I'd be the first person Aspen would call."

While she paced and gestured and talked about possible ways Aspen could make contact, he chewed slowly, reconsidering his theory. "The timing is wrong. Aspen has been missing for five weeks. Why wait until today to come after you?"

Her eyebrows lifted. "Coincidence?"

"It's better to stick with logic."

"You're right," she said. "Why today?"

As she considered, the wheels inside her head began to turn. Her fear dissipated. Using her mind grounded her, and he appreciated that trait. Her sharp intelligence appealed to him more than her *loca* visions.

"Are you ready for my third theory?" he asked.

She sat. "Shoot."

"You keep seeing things that are connected to Vincent Del Gardo—a convicted felon and dangerous man. Also, you led me to that leather necklace. The bad guys could be worried about what else you might figure out."

"How would they know about my visions?"

"We made no secret of contacting you." Using a tortilla, he sopped up the last bit of salsa on his plate. "In one day, you had visits from the sheriff, from me and from my brother, an FBI agent. Even a casual observer would notice."

"So this is your fault."

"A little bit. *Poquito.*"

When he came here this morning, he never expected a *loca bruja* to have valid evidence. However, as the day progressed, he should have been more careful in protecting Emma's privacy. Bringing Dylan to her house had been a mistake.

"Who are these bad guys you keep talking about?" she asked. "I want names."

"Put Del Gardo at the top of the list. He's involved in Julie Grainger's murder."

"Who else?"

"There's a hit man from Vegas—Boyd Perkins. He's after Del Gardo's fortune. Without conscience, he'll kill anyone who gets in his way." He pushed away from the table and stood. "And let's not forget Bridger. Even though you don't think he was the man you saw, he could still be a threat. Let's see if your computer gave us any information on him."

She nodded. "I'd forgotten about the computer search."

So had Miguel. A lot had happened since then.

They returned to her monk-cell office. His nationwide search through crime records had produced seven hits. None of the mug shots matched the man who gave her the hundred-dollar chip.

"That's a relief," Emma said, "because he's coming back tomorrow afternoon. It's good to know that he's not a criminal."

"Or he's using an alias."

She grumbled, "Do you always look on the downside?"

"The positive side comes when we nab *el hombre*. You shouldn't have invited him back."

"I didn't know he might be a bad guy."

"Shouldn't be a problem. I'll be here tomorrow." With the stroke of a couple of keys, he closed down her computer's access to his files. "I should get started on that right away. I want to take the hundred-dollar poker chip to the lab and run fingerprints. Then we'll know for certain if Bridger is a bad guy."

She held the door and waited for him to leave the office. "Whatever you need to do."

In the kitchen again, he turned to face her. "You need to come with me to the lab."

"Tonight?" She shook her head. "I don't think so. I don't usually take Jack out at night."

He shouldn't have to explain. She was smart enough to know what might happen. "It's not safe for you to be home alone."

She glanced at the wall clock. "It's almost nine."

"If I run his prints at the lab and find out that he doesn't have a record, we can eliminate him from the list of suspects."

She glanced toward the baby. "Is it safe for Jack to be in a lab? Aren't there a lot of chemicals?"

The crime lab was spotless—more sanitary than the average bathroom. His boss wouldn't have it any other way. But Miguel couldn't resist teasing Emma. "Dangerous chemicals all over the place. Oh, yeah. Every morning I get up and go to work in a biohazard zone. You should wrap yourself in tin foil, head to toe, before you go inside."

She exhaled an angry huff. "Do you ever stop making jokes?"

"Should I weep? Drip tears down my cheeks, wring my hands and wail?"

"Of course not."

Though he got a kick out of her flares of temper, he was

serious about the threat to her safety. "I'm not laughing when I say you're coming with me."

"It's been a long day," she protested.

He caught her arm and gently pulled her closer. "You need to hear what I'm saying."

"There's nothing wrong with my hearing."

"Then listen." He cupped her delicate chin in his hand, compelling her to meet his gaze. "A sleepy little town like Kenner City isn't supposed to be a place where there are murders, disappearances and threats. But the danger has come here. Just beyond these walls. Just outside these windows."

They were standing so close that he could feel the tension radiating from her as she said, "And I can't run from it."

"You're not alone," he assured her. "I'll be with you. Think of me as your bodyguard."

"Interesting. I've never had anyone guard my body."

"I'm glad to. *Me alegro.*" He gazed down at her beautiful face. Did she even realize how lovely she was? If he stayed this close, he wouldn't be able to resist her. "Bring me the chip Bridger gave you. Remember to hold it on the edges so you won't mess up any fingerprints."

She left the kitchen, and he inhaled a deep breath. At the moment, he wasn't thinking about the chip or the danger or the investigation. Emma filled his mind. He wanted to take her hand and pull her against him, to tangle his fingers in her hair, to kiss her lips.

He didn't entertain these thoughts lightly. He'd never been a *chica* magnet like his twin; he didn't have a string of past girlfriends twenty miles long. When Miguel found himself attracted to a woman, his feelings went deep. Too deep.

Emma returned, holding the chip with her fingers on the edges. Before she could give it to him, she stopped short and frowned. "You again," she said.

Her gaze aimed at the back door. When Miguel looked over his shoulder, he saw nothing. "What's up?"

"It's the bald man with the white beard. He's leaning against the door frame, flipping a gold coin in the air and catching it."

Nothing there. Nothing. *Nada.*

The attraction he'd been feeling came to a screeching halt as he remembered the very good reason why he couldn't get involved with Emma. *Oh, yeah. She's crazy. La loca bonita.*

# Chapter Six

With a resigned sigh, Miguel said, "Tell me about this ghost."

"I guess it makes sense that he'd show up," Emma said. "I have a hundred-dollar poker chip in my hand, and this guy is obviously interested in cash."

Gruffly, he said, "As long as baldy is here, you can ask him a couple of questions."

"Interrogating the dead presents a challenge. They follow their own path with their own agenda, and they don't always choose to cooperate."

Miguel felt his jaw tighten. Not only did he have to put up with ghosts, but he had to respect their rules. "Try mentioning the Centurion Casino."

Staring into empty space, she asked, "Have you ever been to the Centurion Casino in Las Vegas?"

She paused as if waiting for a response. Then she asked, "Does the name Hank Bridger mean anything to you?"

He couldn't believe he was watching her talk to a man who wasn't there. "Is he saying anything?"

"Yes, but it doesn't make sense."

*As if the rest of this made sense?* "Tell me."

"He wants Callie to get what's coming to her."

"Callie? Are you sure he said Callie?"

"I'm positive. He said it again."

Once again, Emma had tapped into a part of the on-going FBI investigation. Callie MacBride was Miguel's boss—the head forensic scientist at the crime lab. She'd testified against Del Gardo. "Who is this bald guy? Ask his name."

She shook her head. "I don't think he's been dead for very long. He's already fading."

"Not yet," Miguel said firmly. "Ask him how he knows Callie."

Emma stared as if mesmerized. "A violent death," she whispered. "Cold. Dark."

"Whose death? Who's going to die?"

"His own death."

"Does he have a name?" He needed to pin this ghost down and make him talk. *Dios mio, could this be more frustrating?* "Emma, who the hell is he?"

"There's something about a crescent moon. He's show-ing me a little flag. There's something on it. A sliver of moon in the upper right corner. And a heraldry symbol."

"Of what?"

"It has the body of a lion and wings." She squinted. "He's coming closer so I can see. Too close."

Cold air blasted over Miguel. Icy fingers reached down his throat and clenched his lungs. What was this? What the hell was going on?

Emma must have felt it, too. Her skin blanched. Though trembling, she staggered toward the baby and leaned down to protect him. But Jack seemed unaffected.

Miguel caught her arms and helped her sit in a chair beside the table. The cold vanished.

"The chill of the dead," she said. "It's unlike any other sensation."

"Are you okay?"

Another shudder wracked her shoulders. "I hate when

they talk about how they died. It's intense. It feels like I'm there with them, like I'm dying."

He held both her hands. Her flesh was ice.

He wanted to warm her, to chase away her fears. He wanted to reassure her that everything was all right. But it wasn't.

Even if he surrounded her with an army of body-guards, she wouldn't be safe. He couldn't protect her from the dead.

AFTER SEEING DOZENS of movies and TV shows with forensic themes, Emma expected the Kenner County crime lab would be a high-tech facility where miracles of deduction were performed using a single speck of lint left at a crime scene. Instead, the lab, which was located on the third floor of an office building, seemed like a rather bland space with several partitions.

Miguel relocked the door as soon as they were inside, standing in a reception area. He picked up the baby carrier by the handle. "Here we are, *mijo*. This is where I work."

"He's impressed," Emma said dryly.

"He should be. We solve crimes here."

She peered around a corner. The lab was mostly dark since it was well after regular working hours. "Where do you keep all the really cool stuff? The spectro-analytic magneto machines?"

"This is a real crime lab. Not a movie." He arched an eyebrow. "We don't have billion-dollar tools. Hey, we don't even have theme music."

"I could hum," she offered.

"Spare me the Mozart."

As she trailed him down the hall, she realized that her concern about dangerous chemicals was utterly unfounded. These tile floors were polished to a high gleam.

Beyond the reception area, Miguel showed her to his half-wall cubicle, equipped with an average-looking desktop computer and a metal bookcase packed with volumes on crime scene analysis. Beside his in-box, piled high with work, was a single-framed photograph—exactly the same family snapshot that his deceased sister, Teresa, had shown her. She took a closer look. There were five children, including Teresa and the twins, Miguel and Dylan. A handsome family, all smiling.

He set the baby seat on the desktop and took a plastic baggie from his pocket. "I'll log this poker chip into evidence."

"Wait." She stepped in front of him. "There's no crime connected to that chip. It needs to be returned. Keeping it would be like stealing."

"Fair enough. I'll run the fingerprints, then give it back to you."

"Is it even ethical to investigate a person's prints without telling them?"

"Sure," Miguel said. "Especially if he's got a criminal record."

A slender, blond woman in a white lab coat came toward them. "Hello, Emma. Do you remember me?"

"Ms. MacBride." She'd brought Jack to Emma's house after Aspen's disappearance.

Miguel said, "This is Callie MacBride."

*Callie?* Her name was unusual; she had to be the same Callie the bald, bearded ghost had mentioned. His voice echoed in her memory. *"I want Callie to get what's coming to her."*

"You're working late," Miguel said.

"There's a lot to do." She peeled latex gloves off her hands, folded them and placed them inside the pocket of her lab coat. Each move was quick and precise. "I've been trying to extract evidence from the leather necklace. I can't believe we missed that clue."

Miguel turned to Emma and said, "Callie is the boss. *El Jefe.* She doesn't like our work to be less than one hundred percent *perfecto.*"

"Forensic science is seldom one hundred percent. I'll settle for ninety-seven. Maybe even ninety-six point four."

"Have you learned anything from the necklace?" Emma asked.

"After being buried in the snow, the fingerprints are too degraded to attempt a match. I checked with Luminol and found no blood trace." Though Callie was talking to Emma, her gaze focused on Jack, who looked especially adorable in his blue snowsuit and knitted cap. "He's grown since I saw him."

"The pediatrician says he's thriving." Emma wanted to get back to the necklace—one of the only clues to Aspen's disappearance. "Is there any way of telling who the necklace belongs to?"

"Not through forensics."

"It'll take research," Miguel said. "Tracking down the maker of the necklace, where it was sold and who bought it."

When Callie moved closer to Jack, Emma sensed the other woman's yearning. "Would you like to hold him?"

Callie needed no further encouragement. She whipped off her lab coat and folded it over the back of Miguel's desk chair. Efficiently, she unfastened Jack's safety belt and lifted him from the chair. He gave her a huge grin, accompanied by cackling noises.

Miguel chuckled. "Ah, *mijo.* He's playing you, Callie."

"He's flirting," Emma said.

"He's beautiful." As Callie snuggled the baby, her features relaxed and her complexion warmed. The cool scientist transformed into an earth goddess. "There's nothing more wonderful than a healthy baby."

Callie's maternal instincts made Emma wonder why she'd never felt that way. Did she lack the mothering hormone? Taking care of Jack hadn't come naturally to her. If she hadn't been able to go online for instructions, she wouldn't have had a clue about how to hold him or change him or feed him.

Nor had she ever experienced a real desire for children. When her friends talked about their biological clocks going off, she'd felt nothing.

Callie rocked on her heels. "You two take care of whatever you need to do. I'll stay with this little one."

Emma placed the satchel with Jack's supplies on the desktop. "He shouldn't be getting hungry for a while, but if he needs anything, it's in here."

"We'll manage." Callie nuzzled the top of Jack's head. "Won't we, sweetie pie?"

Emma hurried to catch up with Miguel, who was already halfway down the hall. He entered a room that reminded her of a high-school science lab with clean countertops, wet sinks and microscopes. The equipment wasn't incredible—not like the array of crime-solving tools she'd seen on television.

Miguel went to one of the stations, opened a drawer and took out a pair of aqua-colored latex gloves. "I want to get the fingerprinting done quickly in case *mijo* decides not to be a sweetie pie, and we have to leave."

She nodded. Though Jack had been behaving like an angel, that behavior could change in two seconds. She perched on a stool beside him and watched as he rolled up the sleeves of his shirt.

"We need to tell Callie," she said. "About the bald man with the beard. We should warn her."

"As soon as I'm done, we'll tell her about the ghost with a vendetta." He snapped on the latex gloves. "Callie can handle it. She's tough. After she testified at Del Gardo's trial in Las Vegas, a hit man came after her. She almost died from smoke inhalation after a fire at the lab."

"Del Gardo, again. He's in the middle of everything, like a spider in his web."

"Things turned out okay for Callie." He removed the chip from the bag. "The FBI bodyguard who was watching her is now her boyfriend. I won't be surprised if they get married."

"And start having babies. Callie looks like she's more than ready for a family." She observed as he lightly dusted the chip. She'd read about the fingerprinting process, but had never seen it done. "What are you doing?"

"Fingerprints leave traces of bodily oil. The powder sticks to them." He held the chip to show her the print. "A unique combination of arches, loops and whorls. We've got at least two distinct prints on this chip."

"One is probably mine," she said. "What comes next?"

"I use tape to transfer the print from the chip to a slide."

Concentrating, he performed this operation. First for one print. Then the other.

Her gaze no longer focused on his hands. She found herself staring at his profile, noticing his firm jaw and full lips. When he concentrated, his eyes narrowed and seemed to glow. His black hair fell carelessly across his forehead.

He stood up straight. "Then I run these fingerprints through AFIS."

"Automated Fingerprint Identification Analysis," she said.

He shot a suspicious glance in her direction. "How do you know about AFIS?"

"Research."

"What kind of research? Tell me about it."

"It's not important." And not something she could share

with him. Usually, she was more careful about keeping her secrets. "Where's this AFIS system?"

"Over here." He led the way to a computer with a large screen. After he accessed the program, he plugged in one of the slides. Half of the screen clearly showed the ridges and whorls of the fingerprint he'd lifted from the chip. The other half was a blur. "Then we wait while the computer compares this print to millions of others."

"You're good at this, Mister Science Guy. How did you get into forensics?"

"I started out in premed. Then I got sidetracked."

As a rule, Emma didn't like to pry into other people's business. Because of her own secrets, she understood the need for privacy. But she was dying to know more about Miguel. Perhaps his interest in law enforcement stemmed from the early death of his sister, Teresa. And what exactly had happened to him? How did he almost die? Why did he wear that medal from Chimayo? "What sidetracked you?"

"If you asked my brother, he'd say I'm too lazy to be a doctor."

"But that's not true."

"How is it that you know me better than my twin?"

She didn't bother running through the obvious deductions. A lazy man wouldn't get through college, follow an intense career, play guitar and fix his motorcycle in his spare time. "Let's just say that a little birdie told me."

"A ghost birdie?"

Teasing, again. "You're such a smart aleck."

"It's my gift."

"Well, it's a very irritating habit." His eyes shimmered. Laughing on the inside? "I don't know whether to punch you in the nose or kiss that smirk right off your mouth."

*Kissing? Why did I say something about kissing?* "I'm sorry. Um, I didn't mean to—"

"Let me make the decision for you." His arm slipped around her waist. With his latex-gloved hand, he brushed the hair off her forehead. "Kiss me."

She had too much on her plate to even contemplate the possibility of kissing. Or a relationship with Miguel? It wouldn't happen, couldn't happen. No matter how appealing he was. "But I—"

"Kiss me, Emma. It's the only way you'll shut me up."

"Oh, well, if I have to…"

She rose up on her toes, intending to give him a peck on the cheek. Her lips betrayed her. At the last second, she turned her head and kissed him full on the mouth, unleashing a flood of sensations that swept through her body and carried her inhibitions away. A lifetime of caution was gone in an instant.

This wasn't meant to be a real kiss, but her arms wrapped tightly around him. Her breasts crushed against his chest.

His lips parted. His tongue flicked against her lips, and she drew him inside her mouth. Happily breathless, she tasted him.

If this was a mistake, she hoped she would err again. A million times.

## Chapter Seven

In the reception area, Emma perched on the edge of a chair beside the boxy sofa where Callie sat with Jack cradled in her arms. Miguel remained standing while he explained to his boss how Emma's visions worked.

She pretended interest in her purple sneakers, not daring to look at Miguel for fear she'd blush. His kiss had surprised her. She wasn't the sort of woman who slipped easily into relationships. Not that she wasn't willing to try, but her lifestyle simply didn't offer many opportunities to meet men. The solitary nature of her work kept her home. The only man she saw on a regular basis was the UPS guy who delivered her online purchases.

And that was okay. She was an introvert; being alone felt natural. And she didn't think of herself as being tragic or lonely. This was simply the way her life had turned out.

At the age when she should have been meeting men and dating, she'd gone to the university in Boulder where there were thousands of available men. But Emma kept to herself. She'd skipped grades and was only sixteen—younger than everybody else. Less experienced and sophisticated, she'd been a skinny, stringy-haired kid who had all the confidence in the world when it came to talking to dead people. But real life? Not so much. Besides, she needed to study furiously to maintain the straight-A average needed for her scholarships.

As a girl growing up on the rez, she'd been an outsider, a teacher's pet, a weirdo who had visions. None of the boys had given her a second glance. Emma had been nothing like her vivacious cousin Aspen, who was popular and always had boyfriends. If only Aspen were here. She'd have some solid advice on what to do about Miguel.

Emma shoved her feelings aside and focused on Aspen. Finding her cousin was all that mattered.

"I understand," Callie said after Miguel's explanation. "Basically, Emma is a medium who contacts people who have passed away."

Emma looked up so quickly that her neck snapped. "I saw a man who spoke of you."

"A man who's dead? Does he have a name?"

"Not that I know."

"What does he look like?" Callie asked.

"Average height and build, maybe with the start of a potbelly. He's completely bald. His beard is white, which makes me think he was older—probably in his early sixties—when he passed. Oh, and he wears black-frame glasses."

Callie shrugged. "Doesn't sound like anybody I know."

"I've seen him twice. He said that he wanted you to get what was coming to you."

"A threat?"

Frowning, Emma recalled the aura surrounding the ghost. "He isn't vengeful. There's something kindly about him. Both times I saw him, he was playing with gold coins. Does that bring up any associations?"

Callie shook her head. "Not a thing."

Miguel said, "Emma sensed that this ghost is recently deceased. Probably murdered."

"That's disturbing," Callie said. She held Jack closer as if to protect him. "How was he killed?"

As was often the case with Emma's visions, the actual circumstances of his death were unclear. The moment of dying seemed to come as a surprise to those who passed on. "Before he died, he was in a cold, dark place. He felt a sudden pain. Maybe he was shot. If I had to guess, I'd say he was attacked from behind."

Jack wiggled in Callie's arms. His nose wrinkled as he started making fussy noises. She stood and rocked him. "Does the baby need a bottle?"

Emma checked her wristwatch. She liked to wait as long as possible before his last feeding so he'd sleep longer. "I should check his diaper first."

"I'll do it," Callie said willingly.

Miguel grinned. "Should I get you a pair of latex gloves?"

"Don't be silly." She unsnapped Jack's outfit. "Miguel, take Emma to the computer with the facial recognition features and put together a composite picture of this ghost."

"Okay."

When he touched her arm to lead her through the lab, her muscles tensed, as if she needed to turn to stone to keep from melting into a puddle of lust and yearning. *What's wrong with me?* This behavior had to stop.

Walking beside him, she straightened her shoulders and tucked her hair behind her ear. She needed to be in control. In a measured tone, she said, "I certainly hope I haven't given you the wrong impression."

"I asked for your kiss. And I enjoyed it, *mi loca bonita.*"

"Your what?"

"*Loca y bonita.* It's what I thought when I first saw you," he said. "It means crazy and beautiful."

He thought she was beautiful. Her spirits soared. "But I'm not crazy."

"Whatever you say." He sat in front of a computer screen and inserted a piece of software. "We use this program instead of a sketch artist. I think it works better. We'll start with the shape of baldy's face."

Though she wanted more of his personal attention, the technology distracted her. She'd used this morphing software before. "Start with an oval."

An oblong appeared on a blank screen.

"His eyes," Miguel said. "Close together or far apart?"

"Hard to tell with his glasses. Average spacing. Kind of squinty. And dark."

An image formed in her mind as she directed him through the other features, adjusting as they went. The emerging sketch reminded her of a Santa Claus caricature. "Can you make him older?"

Using the mouse, Miguel selected a box on the left side of the screen. Wrinkles appeared on the forehead and below the eyes. His cheeks hollowed. "How's that?"

"A little scary." In the blink of an eye, Santa Claus had aged by twenty years and looked like a derelict.

"We use this software with missing persons," he said. "If a kid goes missing at age four, we can get a pretty good indication of what he'll look like at fourteen. Or forty."

"Have you done it on yourself?"

He nodded. "I'm a very distinguished sixty-year-old man. Like a wise professor."

She believed him. Miguel had good bone structure; he'd be one of those men who stayed handsome as he aged. The faint lines at the corners of his eyes would deepen with experience. His cheekbones would be more prominent. And his lips…

She turned her attention back to the sketch. "The picture isn't quite right. His face is a bit leaner. And his nose has a bump, like it was broken."

He adjusted the likeness.

"That's it," she said. "I wish I could do better. With the beard, the bald head and glasses, it's almost like he's wearing a disguise."

Miguel printed the likeness. "Let's see if Callie recognizes him."

In the reception area, Callie stood and swung Jack back and forth. He wasn't screaming but not giggling, either. His forehead pinched in a little-old-man scowl. "I really think it's time for his bottle," she said.

Miguel held up the picture. "Do you know him?"

"He's familiar." She leaned closer, concentrating. "Yes, I've seen him. He was outside my house one night. I remember because he was staring. Watching. But I don't know who he is."

Emma took a bottle of formula from the carry-all. "Should I take Jack now?"

"If you don't mind, I'd love to feed him."

Callie took the bottle and settled comfortably on the sofa. As soon as the nipple touched Jack's mouth, he latched on and slurped with greedy abandon. If Emma hadn't known better, she'd think this baby hadn't been fed in days.

The outer door to the office opened, and a tall, rugged man strode inside. His steely-eyed gaze turned gentle as he beheld Callie with the baby.

She introduced him. "Emma, meet Tom Ryan. My very personal FBI bodyguard."

His huge hand enveloped hers. "Pleased to meet you, Emma. I'll be coming to your house tomorrow with Julie's map."

"You work with Dylan," she said.

"Yes, ma'am." He turned to Callie. "You're seven minutes late."

"Unavoidably detained," she said. "Do you recognize this little guy. It's Jack—Aspen's baby."

"Looking good, Jack." He settled on the couch beside her. Gently, he said, "You're going to have to give him back, you know."

"Of course." Callie looked toward Emma. "Is there anything else you can tell me about the ghost? What about the place where he died?"

"Cold and dark," Emma said.

"A cave," Miguel suggested. "Or a basement."

"That sounds right." She related the other details of her vision. "He showed me a little flag with a sliver of moon and a heraldry symbol. A lion with an eagle's head and wings. I think it's called a griffin."

"Griffin," Miguel repeated with a groan. "As in Griffin Vaughn."

"Makes sense," Callie said.

Miguel turned to Emma. "Griffin Vaughn is a wealthy businessman who bought the house that once belonged to Vincent Del Gardo. It's just outside Kenner City."

"Del Gardo had a house here?"

"The house is probably what brought him to this area after he fled Vegas," Miguel said. "Last month, during the blizzard, Griffin had intruders. Probably men who were looking for Del Gardo's treasure."

"Like Boyd Perkins," she said, recalling the name of the hit man.

"As a matter of fact," Callie said, "we found a finger-print for Perkins at Griffin's house. Maybe your ghost was another of those intruders. You said that he liked to play with gold coins. That suggests a treasure hunter."

"Wait a minute." Tom scowled. "What ghost?"

"I'll explain later," Callie said. "It's complicated."

Emma saw the next step on the path that might lead to

finding Aspen. "We should go to Griffin's house. If that's where the ghost was leading me, I might be able to pick up some kind of clue."

"I concur," Callie said. "I'll arrange it for tomorrow."

"Schedule it for the afternoon," Miguel said. "In the morning, we're going over the map with Dylan and Tom."

Emma's day was filling up. There'd be no time for work, but it didn't matter. One of these clues could lead to her cousin. "I have a regular babysitter who comes in the morning. I'll have to make other arrangements for the rest of the day."

"I'll do it," Callie volunteered. "I'd be delighted to take care of Jack tomorrow."

Emma accepted the offer. One thing she'd learned about babies: you can't have too many babysitters. "We should be getting Jack home to bed. He looks like he's almost done with his bottle."

"Only one thing left to do," Miguel said. "Emma, let's see if AFIS turned up anything on Hank Bridger."

She trotted through the lab behind him, returning to the bland, sterile room where they had shared a kiss. It seemed like the walls should have been colored in passionate pink, but no. Nearing the computer, she recognized the mug shot. "That's him. Hank Bridger."

"That's not the name we have." Miguel tapped a few computer keys. "His original name is Henry Coopersmith, but he's got a string of aliases."

"So he's not an altruistic relative searching for his lost brother?"

"His occupation is listed as professional gambler."

*A Vegas cowboy.* Her first impression had been correct. "Does he have a record?"

"No outstanding warrants, but there's a record. A long

one. He's been charged with assault, robbery and even murder."

And he'd been standing right on her doorstep—only a few feet away from her and Jack. A belated shiver of fear trickled down her spine.

Miguel continued, "This Hank Bridger also has a very good lawyer in Vegas. With all these arrests, he's never been convicted of a crime, never spent one day in the penitentiary. Each time, he gets off. It's not a good pattern."

"Pattern?"

"Arrest charges combined with a slick lawyer, probably an expensive lawyer, suggests that Bridger considers himself above the law and has a big enough bank account to cover his butt." He swung away from the screen and looked at her. "Not many people can make a living as a professional gambler. Makes me wonder what else Bridger is getting paid for."

"Some kind of criminal activity, no doubt. He's very interested in finding the person connected to that poker chip."

He reached out and gently brushed his fingertips from her shoulder to her wrist. He clasped her hand, laced his fingers with hers. "Until we find out what Bridger is looking for, we'll consider him a threat."

"Sure, why not?" She tried to ignore the tingling in her fingertips. "Bridger. Del Gardo. Perkins. Is there anybody in Kenner County who isn't after me?"

"Maybe we should start an Emma Richardson fan club."

"I don't think these guys want my autograph."

She saw a flicker of amusement in his eyes. He slowly grinned. "You're going to be all right."

"Don't promise something you can't guarantee."

"Trust me, Emma. I'll keep you safe."

He squeezed her hand, probably intending to comfort

and reassure her. Instead, she felt an intense urge to run as fast as she could.

Having Miguel as a bodyguard might be more dangerous than facing criminals and hit men. Miguel had the power to shatter her heart.

## Chapter Eight

After they returned to her home, Miguel closed the curtains, locked the doors and took his gun from the holster. He didn't carry a weapon on a regular basis, not like his twin. Dylan was the fighter; Miguel was a lab rat. He'd never actually fired at another human being. There had been confrontations, sure. But showing the gun had always been enough.

*Not this time.* The threat to Emma came from hardcore criminals. Murderers. It would take more than waving a *pistola* to bring them down.

He placed his gun on the spindle-legged table beside the sofa where he'd be sleeping tonight. Since Emma didn't have a guest bedroom, she'd piled sheets, blankets and a fresh towel on the sofa before she retired to her own bedroom to get *mijo* to sleep. Though the baby should have been tired from being out tonight, Jack was still making fussy noises. This would probably be a good time for Miguel to grab a quick shower. He grabbed the towel and went into the bathroom.

On the way to her house, they'd stopped by his little apartment and he'd picked up a couple of essentials: clean clothes for tomorrow, shaving stuff, a pair of pajama bottoms that had never been worn. Miguel slept naked, but he was pretty sure that Emma wouldn't go for that. After that one hot kiss, she'd retreated like a rabbit into the hole.

Standing in the shower with steaming water sluicing over his body, he remembered how she'd felt in his arms, how she'd pulled him closer. She'd tasted sweet, like warm honey. He shook those thoughts from his head so he wouldn't get hard. Emma the Rabbit would burrow even deeper into her hidey-hole if he went strutting through her house with an erection.

Stepping out of the shower, he toweled dry and dressed in the pajama bottoms and a faded black T-shirt. He returned to the front-room sofa.

The baby noises from her bedroom had gone silent. How many times did *mijo* wake during the night? It was after ten o'clock now. Jack would probably need another feeding around three or four. It would be an early morning wake-up call. Not that Miguel was planning on a deep sleep.

As a bodyguard, he needed to be alert enough to hear everything that went on in the house. The sound of glass breaking. The creak of a floorboard. He left the lights in the kitchen and the hallway on. Sometimes, a light was enough to deter an intruder. He made up his bed and stretched out on the sofa.

He'd never been one who required a lot of sleep; a couple of cat naps were enough to sustain him. He rested until a few minutes after two o'clock, when he heard Jack making restless noises.

Rolling off the sofa, he went to the bedroom door and peeked in. The light from the hallway shone on Emma, who was sound asleep in her four-poster bed. Her full lips were parted. Her breathing was steady.

This woman probably hadn't gotten a full eight hours of uninterrupted sleep since the baby came to live with her.

Miguel figured that—since he was already awake—he could give her that gift.

He went to the bassinette beside the bed and lifted the baby into his arms. "Hush, *mijo*. Let Emma sleep."

This was an exercise he'd performed dozens of times for his sisters and cousins. He changed Jack's diaper, went into the kitchen and prepared the formula. Sitting in the rocking chair while he fed the baby, Miguel realized he hadn't been much use tonight as a bodyguard. But as a nursemaid? He was *primo*.

After Jack finished eating, he looked up at Miguel with his big brown eyes. Wide-awake.

"Now's not the time to be cute," Miguel told him.

Jack giggled and waved his arms.

Putting the baby over his shoulder, Miguel began to pace, bouncing with every step. Instead of calming down and going back to sleep, Jack acted like he was on a carnival ride.

Miguel rocked and paced and hummed a lullaby. If he hadn't been concerned about letting Emma sleep, he would have placed the baby in the bassinette and allowed him to fuss for a few minutes before drifting off. That wasn't an option.

With Jack nestled in the crook of his arm, he strolled into Emma's office. Though it wasn't any of Miguel's business, he was curious about the computer research she did in here. Whenever he mentioned her work, she changed the subject. What was it that she did?

He could have opened the desk drawer and looked at the notes she'd been quick to hide when he was in here before, but that seemed too much like spying. Still, there was nothing wrong with studying objects in plain sight.

Her filing cabinets weren't labeled. Without rifling through the papers on her desktop, he saw nothing obvious that pointed to her secrets. He focused on her bookshelf, which seemed to be divided between reference material and fiction.

One entire row was leather-bound classics. Lots of Jane Austen. The only other author who had several hardbacks in a row was Quinn Richards—a bestselling author who wrote hard-boiled spy thrillers.

Jack wiggled, and Miguel brushed a kiss on the baby's head. "Your auntie has a dark side. She likes to read shoot-'em-up books."

Or not. All of these thrillers were in pristine condition, as if they'd never been cracked open. He read the titles: *Ghost of a Chance. Passing for Dead. Code Breaker.*

He took one of the books off the shelf. "Quinn Richards."

Emma had spoken of her grandma Quinn. Her last name was Richardson. Could she have written these books? Sweet, quiet Emma in her pleasant little house?

On the back cover jacket were several quotes about "pulse-pounding adventure" and a head-and-shoulders photograph of Quinn Richards in a black leather jacket. According to the caption, the author was penning his next thriller in an undisclosed location. Like Kenner City?

Miguel studied the photo. Though masculine, there was something familiar about the blue eyes and the high cheekbones.

Earlier tonight, he and Emma had used software to create the accurate picture of the bald ghost. With the touch of a computer key, he could add twenty years to a person's face. Or change them from blond to brunette. Or from a woman to a man. This cover photo was the result of that same kind of morphing.

Quinn Richards was Emma Richardson.

Miguel looked down at the baby, who had finally fallen asleep in his arms. "For now, we'll keep your auntie's secret. Okay, *mijo?*"

THE NEXT AFTERNOON, Emma followed Miguel into the parking lot outside the crime lab where they'd left Jack with Callie.

On this bright, sunny April day with the snow from last month's blizzard mostly melted, the roads were clear and perfectly safe for riding a motorcycle. She had no reason to be scared, but her pulse was racing at a hundred miles an hour—a speed she hoped to only experience in her imagination. The glare from the chrome on his Harley flashed ominously. A death machine. That was what Grandma Quinn always said about motorcycles.

He unlatched the carrier on the back and took out a black helmet with orange-and-red flames. Not a reassuring design.

She looked longingly at her car. "Wouldn't it be safer if we drove?"

He placed the flame helmet in her hands. "I thought we decided it was best to leave your car here in case Callie needed to use the baby seat for Jack."

"I guess we did."

She hoped Callie wouldn't need the car, but better safe than sorry. And Emma was grateful for Callie's offer to babysit while they went to Griffin Vaughn's house to see if the bald ghost's clue had any significance.

Emma didn't have positive feelings about the path their investigation seemed to be following. Earlier this morning, when she'd met with Dylan and Tom Ryan to see if she could pick up anything from the map with the VDG symbol, she'd felt nothing. This piece of paper supposedly came from Agent Julie Grainger, and Emma had expected Julie to appear. No such luck. The map made no sense— just a tangle of scribbles leading to several dead ends.

Dylan had left her with a copy of the map, and she'd traced the lines several times with her finger. Nothing.

After getting a full night's sleep for the first time since

Jack came to live with her, she should have been sharper and more attuned. Instead she was wildly distracted, unable to think clearly—a state of mind that she blamed entirely on Miguel. All her senses seemed to focus on him. Her vision sharpened when she looked at him. Her ears filled with music when she listened to him speak. His scent was like some kind of wonderful, masculine perfume.

Nonetheless, she didn't want to ride on the back of his Harley. "If somebody is really after me, won't I be more exposed on the motorcycle?"

He shrugged. "On the bike, we can make a fast getaway."

*Oh, good.* "What does that mean?"

"Off-road." His voice held the teasing lilt that she was beginning to dread. "We can dash across the hillsides to places where cars can't go. Like a Motocross racer."

"Those guys on motorcycles who swoop twenty feet in the air?" Recalling glimpses of that sport on television, she gasped. "They do flips and they crash, Miguel. They crash hard."

"But you like adventure—pulse-pounding adventure."

What was he talking about? He sounded like a blurb on one of Quinn Richards's book jackets. *Pulse-pounding? Fine, bring it on.* She plopped the helmet onto her head. "I'd like to stop at my house first. It might help if I take the chip from the Centurion Casino with me to Griffin's house."

"How so?"

"When I was holding it last night, the bald man appeared and he's the one who pointed us toward Griffin. If I'm holding the chip, he might come again."

"Whatever you need." His own helmet was a Darth Vader black with a visor. He climbed on and waited for her to mount. "Do you need goggles?"

"Will sunglasses do?"

"*Perfecto.*"

After taking her sunglasses from her purse and draping the strap of the purse across her chest, she slipped onto the black leather seat behind him. "Any other instructions?"

"Hold on to me. Don't wave your arms. Don't jump around."

She wrapped her arms around his torso and leaned against him. In spite of her rampant fear, the full body contact felt wonderful. Her heightened sense of touch made her superaware of his lean strength and the wiry muscles beneath his denim jacket.

He cranked the motor; the Harley roared to life, shuddering beneath her. She tightened her grip, holding on for dear life. Though she told herself to lighten up, she couldn't. Her arms clamped around him in a death grip.

The Harley eased forward in a smooth glide. They were on their way with breezes swirling around them.

She stared at the edge of the road, aware that they weren't moving too fast. If she fell off at this speed, she'd probably only break a couple of bones.

When they halted at a stop sign, Miguel turned his head and asked, "Having fun?"

"Not yet."

But the motorcycle wasn't as scary as she'd expected. Miguel handled the bike with skill—not going too fast and carefully obeying all the traffic rules. By the time they got to her house, she'd relaxed enough to breathe normally. It seemed that she had an instinct for keeping her balance, leaning when he did. When she dismounted, her legs wobbled.

"That wasn't so terrible," she said, taking off her helmet and shaking her hair. "And very practical. Good gas mileage."

"Practical." He flipped up the visor. "That's why Hell's Angels ride Harleys."

"I'll grab the chip and we can be on our way again."

She hurried up the sidewalk, taking her keys from her purse. The main benefit to riding behind him was the close body contact. They fit together perfectly.

Unlocking the dead bolt, she hurried through the front room and dining room. She'd placed the chip in a drawer in her kitchen so it wouldn't get lost in the baby paraphernalia that threatened to consume every flat surface in her house. She pulled open the drawer, reached inside and grasped the chip.

A shape flickered in her peripheral vision.

Before she could turn her head, a rough hand closed around her arm. He yanked her around to face him.

She stared up into the expressionless eyes of Hank Bridger.

## Chapter Nine

Emma should have been terrified. Bridger's rap sheet included murder charges. Even though he was dressed like a dandy—from the rattlesnake band on his hat to his polished snakeskin boots—he was a dangerous man.

But he had broken into her house, violated her personal territory. She was furious.

"Miss Emma," he said, "we had an appointment this afternoon."

"I don't recall setting a time." Her lips pinched together. "Awfully sorry, Mr. Bridger."

"Tell me where to find what I'm looking for?"

"The treasure," she snapped. "Del Gardo's millions."

"That's right." He easily abandoned the pretense that he was searching for his missing brother. "Del Gardo owed me over a hundred grand, and I can prove it. That money is mine. And you're going to tell me where it is."

*Like hell I will.* "How did you get into my house?"

"The back door was open."

*A lie.* She locked the doors before they left. "I'll be happy to return your hundred-dollar chip, but there's nothing more I can tell you."

His grip on her arm tightened. When he leaned close, she could smell his sickeningly sweet aftershave. "I'm a poker player, Miss Emma, and I'm damned good at reading people. I'd advise you to tell me what you know."

He was a huge man. He could break her arm as easily as snapping a twig. But she didn't think Bridger wanted to hurt her. He needed her visions to help him find the money, and he seemed to actually believe that she would do him that favor—track down Del Gardo's millions.

"Do you believe in ghosts, Mr. Bridger?"

His cold black eyes registered no emotion whatsoever. "What do you see?"

Emma cast her gaze to his left. She saw nothing and wasn't a poker player. Still, she bluffed. "There's a ghost beside you. A man who blames you for his death."

When he turned his head and shoulders, the fringe on his jacket bounced. He stared at the empty space where she was looking. "Where?"

"He wants revenge. Can't you hear him wailing? Can't you feel his fiery red eyes staring at you with ultimate hatred?"

He dropped her arm and took a backward step, teetering on the heels of his fancy boots. "I feel nothing."

*Another lie.* His poker face slipped. Bridger might be a cold-blooded, godless thug, but he was superstitious. That was why he came to her in the first place. That was her advantage.

Emma had no weapon. Her physical strength was no match for Bridger. But her imagination was enough to chase him away. "I'm part Ute, Mr. Bridger. I grew up on the rez."

"So?"

"Unless the dead rest easy, they will rise. Like the dreaded Manitou that kills with one blow and devours souls. The Ghost Dancers of my people call forth the dead and they come, seeking revenge from those who wronged them."

He jabbed a finger at her. "Witch. You tell them to leave me alone."

"No one can stop them."

They both heard the front door open. Miguel called out, "Emma, what's taking so long?"

Bridger went to the back door. "This isn't over. When I come back, you'd better have answers for me."

He dashed through the back door, leaving it swinging open on the hinges.

Her threats of undead vengeance clogged her throat, making it hard to breathe. The anger that helped her face Bridger switched to fear. She slid down the cabinets to the floor. With her knees pulled up, she buried her face and whispered a thank-you to her aunt Rose, who had taught her the lore of her people—so many stories of ghostwalkers and the Manitou. Those myths had saved her.

Although afternoon sunlight poured through her kitchen window, darkness wrapped itself around her. The danger she wrote about and imagined in her Quinn Richards books had become her reality. *This is what it's like to face the threat of death.*

She felt Miguel's hand on her trembling shoulders. "Emma, what's wrong?"

"Bridger. He was here, waiting for me."

"Where did he go?"

"Out the back door." She lifted her head. "Only a minute ago."

Miguel rose, went to the door and stepped outside. She noticed the gun in his hand. A new terror propelled her to her feet. Bridger's superstitions would keep him from harming her, but Miguel had no such protection.

He stormed back into the house, grasped her hand and kept moving, dragging her behind him toward the front door. "I think we can catch him."

"What? On the motorcycle?"

"That's right."

As she stumbled after him, her battered emotions—the terror and the rage—coalesced into one word. "No."

"I can't leave you here alone," he said as they approached the Harley. "Put on your helmet."

"A helmet decorated with the flames of hell? No."

"I want to see what kind of vehicle he's driving. To get his license plate number." He placed the helmet on her head. "Get on."

"There won't be any shooting?"

"Not from me."

Against her better judgment, she climbed onto the back of the Harley. Surely, there were easier ways to get a license plate number, like checking with motor vehicle registration. But Bridger was the king of aliases. His car could be registered under any number of names. There had to be—

Her mind went blank as Miguel swooped down her driveway into the street. The sheer power of the Harley shuddered through every muscle in her body. Holding on took all her strength. She was riding on the back of a rocket.

The familiar sights of her neighborhood whirled past in a wild collage. She saw the tall spruce tree on the corner. Oh, God, they were going to hit the tree.

Miguel turned fast. Disaster averted.

But she was slipping. Her sense of balance was gone. Her clumsy weight would cause them both to fall. To crash and burn.

He circled her block, darted a few streets to the west. Then back.

Then he stopped. "Got it. He's driving a black SUV. I got the plates."

She could only make a small peep.

"Are you okay back there?"

She peeped again.

"Hang on. We're going back to your house."

In just a few moments, they were in her driveway again. Emma caught her breath and climbed off the shiny, chrome beast. From her scalp to her toenails, she was trembling. It took an effort to remove the helmet, walk to her front door and collapse on the sofa in the front room.

While she caught her breath, Miguel strode through her house, making sure no one else was hiding in a closet. He came back and squatted down in front of her. "You did good, Emma."

"I thought I was going to die."

He winced. "I never should have let you come into the house by yourself."

His expression was contrite. She didn't tell him that facing Bridger had been far less terrifying than their wild ride. "I'm all right."

"It's time to find you a real bodyguard, instead of a lab rat. My brother never would have made such a mistake."

"Don't blame yourself."

"Who else? I see no other *estupido* in this room."

*"Estupido?"*

"Idiot. Moron." He took out his cell phone. "I'm calling the sheriff. With a license plate number, he might be able to pick up Bridger and bring him in for questioning."

"Good."

"Then we'll find you another guard."

She didn't want a different bodyguard. Miguel made her feel safe while at the same time not restricting her. When he disconnected the call, she stood on shaky legs and said firmly, "I want you."

"You do?"

"I want you to be my bodyguard. I trust you, Miguel. I can't have someone hovering over me, waving a gun."

He moved closer. "If anything had happened to you—"

"But it didn't." She touched his cheek, reassuring herself

with his nearness. "My mind needs to be free and uncluttered if I hope to have more visions. I need to see. It's the only way I'll find Aspen."

"You're a good woman, Emma."

"And a pain in the neck. A burden."

"A precious burden."

He enfolded her in his arms and pressed his mouth against hers. His strength absorbed her shivering fear. His intimate touch roused a passion she'd never experienced before. She wanted him. In every possible way.

ALTHOUGH EMMA SAID she could manage the rest of the ride to Griffin Vaughn's house on the Harley, Miguel called on his twin for help. Dylan showed up with his vehicle, which Miguel drove with Dylan in the passenger seat, keeping an eagle eye on the road ahead and the surrounding area. Emma sat in back.

In spite of her reassurances that he was a good bodyguard, he knew he'd made a mistake. Never should he have allowed her to enter her house alone. The thought of her alone with Bridger turned his blood to ice. The bastard could have killed her.

Nor would he be casual about the installation of burglar alarms at her house. He told her to cancel the appointment she'd made with a Durango-based company who promised to be out tomorrow afternoon. Not fast enough! Miguel arranged with Bart Fleming from the lab to set up a security system today.

Miguel wouldn't take any more chances with her safety. She was more to him than a mere witness, much more. He hadn't felt this way about a woman in years. Maybe ever.

He concentrated on the road ahead, constantly checking his rearview mirror in case they were followed.

"You're jumpy as a cat," Dylan said.

"Staying alert."

"Relax, *vato*. You've got it under control. Everything is okay."

Easy for him to say. Dylan had been trained in protecting witnesses. This job was new for Miguel.

Dylan glanced over his shoulder toward Emma. "Let me get this straight. Bridger told you that he was after Del Gardo's treasure."

"That's right."

"And he thinks you know where it's hidden."

"But I don't," she said. "I can't imagine where anybody could hide fifty million. That has to be a truckload of cash."

Miguel agreed. "Del Gardo can't be carrying around that fortune with him. He's had plenty of time to convert the money. It could be precious gems. Or certificates of deposit."

His brother was quick to refute. "An amount that large would trigger alarms. The FBI has no record pointing to any such transaction."

"Use your imagination, *vato*." Miguel resented the way Dylan thought the FBI knew everything. In this case, they were as stymied as the Kenner County sheriff's department. "Del Gardo could have loaded his cash on a plane and flown to an offshore bank."

"Oh, sure." Dylan scoffed. "There he was—in a tropical paradise with enough money to last more than a lifetime, then he turned around and came back here. Why? And why did Julie make a map?"

"Maybe he stayed on that tropical island," Emma said. "Are you sure he's in Kenner County?"

"Bridger seems to think so," Dylan said. "So does Boyd Perkins. Just a few weeks ago, Miguel found Perkins's fingerprints at Griffin Vaughn's house. That happened during the blizzard when Griffin and his assistant, Sophie, were snowed in."

In the distance, Miguel spotted Griffin Vaughn's home. Perched on a hillside above an outcropping of rock, it was a modern structure, two stories, with wraparound windows. "Almost there."

Emma craned forward. "Wow! That's quite a house."

With the money she made as Quinn Richards, the best-selling writer of thrillers, she could probably afford a place like this. Instead, she chose to live in her cozy little home and pretend to be nothing more than a researcher. When the time was right, he'd find out why. "Griffin is a million-aire businessman from California."

"Why would he move here?" she asked. "I mean, the house is spectacular. But Kenner County?"

"Haven't you noticed?" Dylan chuckled. "Everybody in California wants a second home in Colorado."

Miguel added, "It's a place where they can escape after the San Andreas fault breaks apart and an earthquake drops L.A. into the Pacific."

Dylan nudged his arm. "All those California guys want to be cowboys like us."

"Some *vaquero* you are. When was the last time you were on a horse?"

"I can ride. Better than you." He looked back toward Emma. "When he was a kid, my brother got thrown from a sway-back mule."

Miguel launched into his own story about how Dylan tried to impress a girl by signing up for bull-riding at a local rodeo. As he told Emma about Dylan's spectacular failure and how he walked with a limp for a week, Miguel's spirits lifted. Picking at his twin felt normal and right.

The door to Griffin's home was answered by Sophie LaRue, his executive assistant who was about to take a more permanent job as Griffin's wife. She was a pretty woman with blond hair and a bright smile.

"Come on in," she said. "Griffin and his son are out, but if there's anything I can do to help, name it."

Miguel wasn't sure what they were looking for, and he didn't want to tell Sophie that they'd been sent here by a ghost. After he introduced Emma, he peeked toward the living room. "You've made some improvements since the last time I was here."

"You know how it is when everything is under construction." Sophie beamed at Emma. "One day, it's chaos. Then next, voila."

She made a sweeping gesture with her hand, nearly knocking a vase off its pedestal.

"Your home is beautiful," Emma said. "Classic."

"She likes classic," Miguel muttered to his brother.

"And you like her," he whispered back. "Remember, *vato*. I'm best man at your wedding."

"And you get your pick of the prettiest bridesmaid."

They watched as the two women oohed and aahed over the view and the new furnishings. Finally, Miguel stepped forward. "I think we need to see the basement."

"Right," Emma said. "A cold, dark place."

"It's still a mess," Sophie said. "But come along."

Emma hesitated. She was staring at a space near the entrance. Nothing there.

Neither Dylan nor Sophie noticed anything odd about her behavior, but Miguel knew what was happening to Emma. She was following one of her ghosts.

## Chapter Ten

Descending the staircase into the basement of Griffin's house, Emma shivered. The chill of the dead.

The first time she'd seen Julie Grainger, the murdered woman's presence had been faint. Her voice, a mere whisper. Now her spirit was stronger. Her FBI jacket flapped around her as she darted back and forth, coming too close for Emma's comfort. Anxiously, she beckoned. "This way, this way."

Emma picked her way through the basement. The construction work that had been finished so beautifully in the upstairs was in progress down here. Concrete pylons leaned against half-finished walls. Piles of debris cluttered the cement floor.

Trying to do as Julie instructed, Emma moved deeper into the mess. The cold sank into her bones. The only light came from bare bulbs hung across the ceiling. Shadows loomed all around her.

When Miguel came close behind her, she was glad for his presence and his warmth. "You're following someone," he said. "Is it baldy again?"

She shook her head. "It's Julie."

He winced. "Don't tell Dylan. He still mourns her passing."

Julie's voice intruded. "I'm sorry," she said. "I brought heartache to my friends. I'm so sorry."

Her comment startled Emma. The people she saw in her visions didn't usually acknowledge anyone else. They spoke only to her and often in riddles. In life, Julie must have been an exceptionally straightforward person.

"Tell him," Julie said. "Tell Dylan not to grieve. Let him know I'm all right. Beyond pain, beyond sorrow."

Emma whispered in Miguel's ear. "She wants Dylan to know that she's fine. And she regrets causing him pain."

Dylan tromped up behind them. "Hey, are you telling secrets?"

Miguel held up his hand as if to forestall any teasing from his brother. "I'll tell you later."

In spite of their constant verbal jabs, these twins had an obvious bond of understanding. Their expressions mirrored each other. Dylan immediately comprehended the gravity of the situation. "I can wait."

Sophie stumbled beside them, catching herself before she fell. In her hand, she held a huge flashlight. "Where are we going?"

Emma pointed the way, trailing Julie as she wound around unfinished walls. Taking a quick turn, the ghost disappeared behind a concrete pylon.

Emma hurried to catch up. The others followed.

Julie stood beside a concrete slab that leaned against one of the outer walls of the basement. A stack of old timber from the demolition had been piled in this corner.

Faintly glowing, Julie said, "This is what you're looking for. This is your path."

The path to finding Aspen? Emma could only hope that they were headed in the right direction. Something in this basement could lead to her cousin.

"Dig here," Julie said. "Keep digging."

Like a wisp of smoke, she vanished.

Shivering, Emma pointed. "Here. Dig here."

Sophie came up beside her. "Are you all right?"

This charming woman had been given zero explanation about what they were doing there or about Emma herself. She looked into Sophie's guileless eyes. "I should tell you a few things about me."

While Miguel and Dylan dug through the debris, Emma explained her abilities as a medium. Sophie nodded calmly. She was one of the least judgmental people Emma had ever met.

"I'm not surprised," Sophie said. "I thought there might be ghosts in this house."

"You're quick to accept."

"I'm from California." Mimicking a brainless beach beauty, she fluffed her blond curls. The pose didn't suit her; Sophie was much too intelligent to play dumb. "Half the people I know have regular appointments with psychics. Mostly charlatans. But you're the real deal, aren't you?"

"Afraid so." She was quick to add, "I can't see the future. I don't do counseling and I don't make my living from my visions."

Sophie nodded. "What kind of work do you do?"

"Consulting and research. I work from home on my computer."

The familiar lie slipped easily through her lips. Emma wished she could tell her real profession. Not that she wanted the praises that were sure to be heaped onto Quinn Richards, the bestselling thriller writer. But she liked Sophie and wished she could be honest with her. "And you? You're an executive assistant to Griffin Vaughn?"

"I was. But we fell in love." A simple declaration, spoken with heartfelt tenderness. "We're going to be married."

"Congratulations." If Griffin shared her passion, Emma would venture an obvious predication: these two would be happy together.

"Hey, Emma." Miguel called to her from the pile of clutter that he and his brother were taking apart piece by piece. "Are you sure this is the right place?"

"Positive."

"Aim that flashlight over here."

Sophie moved closer and focused the light on the stack of old wood. As Miguel and Dylan worked, dust kicked up around them. Tiny motes swirled and danced in the bright beam that cut through the semidarkness.

"If you don't mind my asking," Emma said, "why did you think there were ghosts here?"

"The man who built this house was that Las Vegas mobster, Vincent Del Gardo. A convicted felon. I think he brought a lot of bad karma in here with him."

Bad karma made sense to Emma. Her aunt Rose often did a smudging ceremony to purify their house on the rez, burning sage and other herbs in an earthen bowl and using the smoke to chase away negative thoughts or presences.

If she and Sophie became friends, she'd offer to do that ceremony. Right now, Emma had other concerns. Finding Del Gardo seemed to be key. He could lead her to Aspen. If she touched something that had belonged to him, it might call forth another spirit to point her in the right direction. "Did Del Gardo leave anything behind?"

"Bits and pieces," Sophie said. "This basement was his wine cellar. Some of this scrap wood is from the racks."

She doubted that holding the splinters would be useful. "Sometimes when I touch something that belongs to a person, I can pick up a sense of where to find them."

"Terrific." Again, Sophie readily accepted a statement

that many people might consider outrageous. "I'd feel a lot better if I knew Del Gardo was in custody."

"Did he leave any of his belongings?"

Sophie thought for a moment before speaking. "There was the wine itself. A whole case of it. Griffin and I opened a bottle. I'm no connoisseur, but I could tell it wasn't very good."

"A wine bottle probably won't help me. I need something more personal."

"Oh, this wine was personal. He was bottling it himself. There was a symbol on the label—a bunch of vines twisted around his initials. VDG. Vincent Del Gardo."

Emma blinked. Sophie had just given her the explanation for the symbol she'd drawn in a trance—the symbol on Julie's map. "We have to tell Dylan about this."

Before Emma could interrupt the brothers, Miguel made a discovery of his own. He held up a wooden plaque, eight inches square. Burned into the wood was the VDG symbol.

"That's it," Sophie said. "That logo was on the labels of Del Gardo's wine."

Miguel and Dylan exchanged a glance. Though they weren't identical, their expressions matched. Simultaneously, they shook their heads.

"A wine label," Dylan muttered.

"Look at the vines," Miguel said. "It's obvious. You should have figured this out before."

"Me? You're supposed to be the smart one."

"When I have all the facts," Miguel said. "Did you know Del Gardo made wine?"

"Does it matter, *vato?*"

Emma spoke up, repeating Julie's words. "Keep digging."

Miguel turned toward her and held up the plaque. "Isn't this what we were supposed to find?"

"It's a clue, but there's more. A path."

They went back to work, clearing the area until there was only one large slab of concrete leaning against the wall.

Dylan smacked the flat of his hand against it. "We can't move this without a crane."

Miguel reached into the narrow space behind it, feeling against the wall. "There's something back here. It's wood."

They juggled the flashlight between them, trying to see what was behind the slab. After much discussion, they decided the best thing was to try to move it. One twin stood on each side. They braced themselves. As soon as they touched the slab, the concrete moved easily. Both men jumped back.

Emma covered her mouth to keep from laughing out loud.

"Fake rock," Dylan said. "It's lightweight."

Miguel checked the floor. "There are rollers on the bottom. It's on a track."

He shoved the concrete aside, revealing a small wooden door, only five feet tall.

Dylan jiggled the door handle. There was no lock, and it opened smoothly on well-oiled hinges. *"Dios mio,"* he said as he ducked and stepped inside. The darkness swallowed him, then he popped back out. "It's a tunnel."

Miguel was right behind him. "Looks like Del Gardo made himself an escape hatch when he built this house. If the law came looking for him, he'd have a getaway."

"And a way back inside," Sophie said. "When we were snowed in, this must be how the intruders gained access. Del Gardo himself could have been hiding down here."

Miguel took a pair of latex gloves from his pocket and slipped them on. "I don't have enough gloves to go around. The rest of you, don't touch anything."

Sophie moved to the front of their little group. She shone the flashlight into nearly impenetrable darkness.

Emma had been looking for a path. Grandma Quinn told

her to follow the trail. This tunnel had to lead somewhere. Entering seemed like the right thing to do.

But something held her back. She heard Julie's voice. A whisper. One word. "Murder."

MIGUEL HAD REALLY WANTED to explore the secret passageway. As a crime scene, that tunnel presented forensic challenges he'd never face again. Not to mention the potential for uncovering a hell of a lot of evidence. Besides which... it was cool. What guy wouldn't want to crawl around in a mobster's getaway tunnel?

But Emma came first. She'd pulled him back from the entrance, insisting there was something else they needed to do first. A different direction they needed to take.

Miguel had no choice. As her self-appointed bodyguard, he had to stay with her. He'd called in other experts from the crime lab.

Upstairs in Griffin's house, he paced in the living room while Emma stood, glowering through the panoramic windows, impatient to get started. One of her ghosts had given her a new lead, and she wanted to get on it. *Too bad.* Before they went anywhere, Miguel needed to do his job.

Via radio transceiver, he was in communication with the team from the crime lab—Bobby O'Shea and Ava Wright. They'd raced over here as soon as he called and were already making their way through Del Gardo's tunnel. According to what they told him, a narrow bore led from the wood door in the basement and ran for approximately fifty yards before hooking into the twisting tunnels of an underground mine.

Bobby's voice came through Miguel's receiver. "It appears that somebody's been living down here. There's a bedroll, a trash bag, some clothes, discarded water bottles."

"How's the air?" Miguel asked.

"Not bad. There must be shafts to let in fresh air, but I don't see them. When we turn off our high-beam lanterns, it's total darkness. I mean, totally. You can't see an inch in front of your nose."

"No messing around, Bobby. Don't turn off the lights."

"This place is incredible." Bobby was young, inexperienced and enthusiastic. "Like being in the bat cave."

Ava spoke up. "Don't worry, Miguel. Everything is under control. I'm recording our progress on video. And taking lots of pictures."

"Be sure to document the bedroll and keep going. See where the tunnel leads."

"There's a fork ahead," she said. "We're on an incline. We'll go right."

"Keep me posted."

These old mines were dangerous. There could be cave-ins or rock slides. He was glad his crew came equipped with hard hats, gloves and heavy coats.

Emma pivoted on her heel and stalked toward him. "Are you done yet?"

He was sick and tired of jumping every time a ghost said boo. "What's the hurry?"

"It's almost sunset." She gestured toward the windows. "We need to take care of this before dark."

All she'd told him was that this direction was important. He'd resigned himself to the fact that his scientific training and expertise had proven to be less effective than her visions. But he wanted some details. This time, he needed a solid sense of what the hell he was getting himself into. "Take care of what, Emma? What are we looking for?"

She lowered her voice. "I didn't want to mention Julie in front of Dylan, not until you've had a chance to talk to him."

"What did Julie tell you?"

"Murder. That was all she said. Murder." Her full lips pursed. "After that, I had a series of impressions. A road leading away from the house. Three pine trees up on a hill. The VDG symbol. And a crescent moon like the one on the flag baldy showed to me."

Nice list. Murder, road, trees, VDG, moon. Might as well wrap it up with a partridge in a pear tree. "What does it mean?"

"Here's what I think." She spread her hands as if laying out a tidy explanation. "Del Gardo killed somebody and left the body near those trees. As for the moon? I don't know."

These guessing games were driving him crazy. Why couldn't her visitors from the other side be more direct? "But you didn't actually see a body."

"Well, no."

"Julie could have been talking about her own murder."

"I suppose so."

From his receiver, he heard Bobby's voice. "We took a couple of wrong turns. We're back where we started."

Miguel turned on the speaker button. "Try again."

"We need to mark the turns we're taking. Or maybe we could get a really long string to roll out behind us."

"Or leave a trail of bread crumbs like Hansel and Gretel." Miguel couldn't keep the sarcasm from his voice. "Don't mess up the crime scene."

"Got it."

He turned back to Emma. "I should be with them. The tunnels are a real source of evidence. I could be looking at facts, fingerprints and DNA. Julie led us there for a reason."

"Then she pointed me in a different direction." She showed no sign of backing down. "If you don't want to come with me, I can follow this lead by myself."

"I won't leave you unprotected." Not after what happened the last time.

"I'm not in danger from Bridger. He's a superstitious man who thinks I know where Del Gardo's treasure is hidden. He's not going to hurt me until he finds out what I know."

"So he's not going to kill you," he said. "All he might do is abduct you and force you to tell him about the treasure."

"Force me?"

"Break your arm. Shoot off your kneecap. Maybe cut off your fingers."

The worry lines between her fine eyebrows deepened. "I hadn't thought of that."

Of course, she hadn't. Reality wasn't her thing.

Emma wasn't an investigator. She was a woman who wrote novels about crime where the bad guys were always caught and the good guys never got injured. She talked to dead people and turned up clues for other people to investigate.

"Here's another reason I can't leave you alone," he said. "Boyd Perkins? He's probably the first person who tried to break into your house. You remember that, don't you?"

"Of course."

"And Perkins is a cold-blooded killer."

"But he doesn't want me. He's after Aspen."

"Do you think he'd leave you alive? He kills witnesses."

He saw fear in the tightening of her jaw and the darting of her eyes, but she remained determined. "I have to take the risk. This could be the next step toward finding my cousin."

If she was right and there was a body hidden nearby, they'd be smart to locate the corpse before dark. Miguel knew from experience that night predators could do a lot of damage to a crime scene. "We'll follow your lead. But only for half an hour."

"Fair enough." Her features relaxed, and she gave him a dazzling smile. "Thank you, Miguel."

His gaze lingered too long on her lips before he blinked and purposely looked away. He'd be a fool to let her know how easily she could charm him into doing whatever she wanted. All it really took was a smile from her, and he caved.

He followed her to the door. *Vamanos. Let's go. Off on another wild ghost chase.*

## Chapter Eleven

Driving his brother's car, Miguel crept along a rutted dirt road that circled away from Griffin's house into rugged mountain terrain. The road narrowed to one lane—not much more than a ledge carved into the rock. He glanced toward Emma. "In your vision, did you see me busting the axle on Dylan's car?"

"I don't predict the future," she reminded him.

"Right." That would make life too easy. At least, this road was on the sunny side of the cliff, which meant all the snow from the blizzard had melted and there was no ice to contend with.

She stared past him through the driver's window toward the arid valley that spread below. "I miss Jack," she said.

"First time you've been away from him?"

She nodded. "Callie would call if there was anything wrong. Right?"

"The only problem might be prying sweetie pie Jack from her arms. We'll pick up the baby after Bart Fleming gets here. He called and told me he's almost done with the burglar alarm system at your house."

"You're coming home with me? I thought you were going to stay here and investigate the mine shaft."

"I stay with you." How many times did he have to tell her? "I'm beginning to think you don't want me around."

"Not true." Her hand rested lightly on his arm, then withdrew quickly. A shy touch. Like a feather in the wind. "You make me feel safe."

And he liked that she felt like that. He'd never been a protector before. "What made you think of Jack?"

"This land. These valleys and mountains. I want Jack to connect to his birthright as a Ute. Aspen would have wanted him to…" She caught herself. "She'll be back. She'll be able to introduce Jack to the land where his ancestors were born."

He wished he could reassure her.

Through the receiver, he heard Ava's voice from the tunnels. "Miguel, I think we're finally headed in the right direction."

"Toward the exit?" he asked.

"You wouldn't believe all the twists and turns. We're going to need a map of this mine system."

"Some of the old silver mines in this area date back to the 1800s," he said. "Those old prospectors made up the rules as they went along, jumping from one vein to another until the ore played out."

He thought there might be a GPS program to map the underground tunnels. "Get back to me when you find the entrance."

"Ten-four," Ava said.

The road ahead branched into a fork. Miguel stopped the car and turned to Emma. "Which way? High or low."

"I'm not sure. The road going up looks a little wider."

He revved the engine and climbed, hoping he'd find a turnaround at the top. Backing down this road would be hell. As he reached a wide level spot, she pointed. "There. Those are the three trees."

He climbed out of the car and trudged behind her as she hiked up the gravelly hillside. The odds against finding a body hidden in the mountains were astronomical. He'd worked with search-and-rescue teams before. Even using heat-sensing scanners and helicopter surveillance, they often failed to locate people who disappeared. This rugged land reclaimed the dead, turning dust to dust.

Emma reached the trees. Standing under the spreading boughs, she rested her hands on the trunk as if to draw a signal from the roughened wood. He didn't question her process; she got results.

As he joined her, she turned in a slow circle. This behavior was new. "What are you doing, Emma?"

"Looking for a crescent moon. Maybe there's a piece of jewelry. Or half of a wheel rim."

In his investigations, Miguel was accustomed to searching for details. He'd developed an ability to focus, shining a mental spotlight on the scene of a crime. The earth beneath their feet was soft, still holding moisture from the recent snows. Only a few yards away, he saw a footprint.

Cautiously, he approached the perfect indentation of a square-toed cowboy boot. Larger than average, it was probably a size thirteen or even fourteen. Boyd Perkins was a tall man, over six feet. As was Bridger. Either one of them might have made this print.

Emma stood beside him. "Looks like somebody besides us has been here."

"It's a good print. We'll make a cast of it. Be careful not to mess it up."

He looked in the direction the toe was pointing. Finding such a precise print was an anomaly in the wilderness, but he made out another heel. And another.

Looking ahead, he saw broken branches on a shrub. Signs of a scuffle. "Stay back, Emma."

Being careful not to disturb anything in the immediate

area, he studied the ground, the pine needles, the vegetation. "Blood."

Across the flat surface of a rock, he saw a smear. Though he wouldn't be sure until he tested, it looked like dried blood. Emma's theory about a murder taking place was gradually being backed up by physical evidence. "There was a struggle here."

"But no body," she said.

He climbed a few steps higher. A fresh nick on the bark of a pine trunk could have been caused by a bullet. He turned a hundred and eighty degrees and stared down the hill.

"What are you seeing?" she asked.

"Ironic." He laughed out loud. "You're asking me what I'm seeing?"

"I am."

"Gathering evidence," he said. "I'm trying to piece together what happened here."

"Well? What happened?"

"I can't be sure. I don't like to make an analysis until I have all the facts."

"Give it a shot." She gave him a wry grin. "I make deductions from almost nothing."

"Which is why we're different," he said. "It seems to me that one man was in pursuit of the other. They struggled. The pursuer pulled a gun and fired. The man being chased continued, trying to get away. But why was he running uphill?"

"Why not?"

"If someone was coming after me with a gun, I'd try to put distance between us. Going downhill is faster." He turned again and looked uphill. "Unless he was running toward something."

The late afternoon sunlight slanted through the trees and deepened the shadows on the rocks. On the flat surface of a heavy boulder, a concave groove etched a shadow in the shape of a crescent. "Do you see it?"

"The crescent moon."

Together, they approached the boulder. The land had been recently disturbed. Branches were torn from shrubs. Stones were overturned, their muddy side facing up. The debris piled against a crevasse on the left side of the crescent boulder.

He shoved aside one of the rocks, revealing part of a leg and a foot in a running shoe.

His fingers itched to tear these rocks apart, but he'd wait for a proper deconstruction of the crime scene. Even if the killer had been wearing gloves, he'd leave traces of evidence.

Emma gasped. "It's a grave."

For someone who routinely hung out with the dead, she seemed shaken. Her arms wrapped around her waist, and she shuddered.

"You're frightened," he said.

"I've never seen a murder victim before. Not in the flesh."

It never got easier. Though Miguel kept his emotions hidden behind an attitude of scientific detachment, he felt empathy for the victims. In his investigations of crime scenes, he always treated the deceased with respect.

Glancing down, he realized that his hand had closed around the silver medallion he always wore around his neck. Silently, he offered a prayer. *May this dead man rest in peace.*

"I know who it is," Emma said. "The bald man with the beard."

"Is he here? Do you see him?"

"No, but I sense him. He suffered before he died. Attacked from behind."

He remembered what she'd told him about baldy's death. "You said he was in a cold, dark place."

"I must have been wrong."

From the hillside above them, Miguel heard a shout. He looked up and saw Ava and Bobby. Looking down from a ledge, still wearing their hard hats, they waved and shouted. "Miguel, what are you doing here?"

He might ask the same question. "Is this where the mine tunnel comes out?"

"This is it. The entrance to the abandoned silver mine."

*A cold, dark place.* Miguel recast his thinking. If the bald man had been concentrating on those tunnels when he died, it would explain Emma's impression of cold and dark. "He was running *toward* the mine."

"To escape," she said. "The mine was his destination, his safe haven."

"Which explains why he was running uphill."

This simple piece of the puzzle was answered. Now, Miguel faced the big question: who was he running from?

EMMA FELT GUILTY for pulling Miguel away from both scenes of investigation—the tunnels and the grave. But she was glad that he'd come home with her and Jack. Finding the body was an uneasy reminder that these men—Boyd Perkins, Hank Bridger and Vincent Del Gardo—were capable of murder.

The newly installed security system at her house should have made her feel more protected. Not only did it blast an alarm if anyone tried to break a window or open a door, but there were also surveillance cameras at the front and back door. Also, Sheriff Martinez had promised to have a patrol car cruising regularly through her neighborhood.

Lots of people were keeping an eye on her, but she still looked to Miguel as her protector. His presence made her feel safe. In the meantime, as a bonus, she had the pleasure of his company.

They'd already cleaned up after dinner, which was a simple matter of dumping paper plates since they'd ordered in a pizza. In the living room, she spread a quilt on the floor and placed Jack in the center on his back. His tiny legs kicked in time to Mozart from the CD player.

Sitting in the rocking chair, she glanced toward the kitchen, where Miguel was on his cell phone, talking to Callie from the crime lab. Emma saw Grandma Quinn standing in the doorway, waggling her finger in a chiding motion.

Emma heard Grandma's voice inside her head. *Babies shouldn't be on the floor. There are germs.*

In a quiet voice, Emma replied, "Jack needs to be in different places, with different things to stimulate him."

*Who told you that?* Grandma huffed.

Though she'd read about stimulating baby's senses in one of the baby books she'd purchased online, Emma wasn't about to tell Grandma that she preferred the advice of experts. Instead, she looked up and asked, "What do you think of Miguel?"

Grandma patted her hair as if primping. In her day, she'd been a beauty. *A handsome fellow.*

"I've kissed him. Twice."

*Good for you, Emma.*

As Miguel strode into the room, Grandma vanished.

He squatted down on the floor beside Jack but looked up at her. "I heard you talking."

Not wanting to relay the message that her deceased grandma thought he was cute, she said, "Chatting to Jack."

"Whatever you say, *loca bonita.*" He turned his attention to the baby. "You're getting a workout, *mijo.*"

"I hope he'll tire himself out before bed," she said. "What did Callie tell you?"

"The dead man had a shaved head and white beard. From his premortem bruising, he appeared to have been in a fight before he was shot in the back, three times. Estimated time of death was forty-eight hours ago."

The bald man had been dead before Emma had her vision about being chased by a man with a knife and her psychic floodgates opened. There must be a connection between Aspen's disappearance and the dead man. "Do they know his name?"

"No identification yet." Miguel picked up one of Jack's toys—a brightly colored plastic rattle—and jiggled it over the baby's grasping fingers. "They'll get started right away on a preliminary autopsy. Once the crime lab has the bullets, we'll know more. Our ballistics expert is *primo*."

Oddly enough, his crime lab shop talk about autopsies and ballistics didn't seem out of place while he played with the baby. "Did they find other evidence near the grave?"

"No fingerprints. The killer must have been wearing gloves." He tickled Jack's tummy. "They've got samples of the dried blood and made a cast of the boot print, which doesn't do us much good until we have a boot to compare it to."

"But the boot print didn't match the dead man?"

"No. Must have been the killer. It's a size-thirteen boot, so he's probably a big guy. Like Bridger or Perkins. Not Del Gardo. He's average height."

"But still dangerous," she said.

"When a man is holding a gun, size doesn't matter."

When Miguel glanced up at her, Emma lost her train of thought. As Grandma Quinn noted, he was a handsome fellow. Even after the long, strenuous day they'd had, his green eyes were sharp and alert. He didn't look tired at all. A teasing smile played on his lips.

She sank to her knees on the floor beside him. As he spoke, she watched his mouth, not really hearing his words as he talked about Del Gardo and his secret tunnel leading from the silver mine into the house he'd built.

The room had gone quiet, except for the noises Jack

made, and she realized that Miguel was looking back at her as if expecting a response. She had no idea what he'd been talking about. She cleared her throat. "Did they find evidence in the tunnels?"

"I just told you that."

"Sorry, my mind was wandering."

"They found clothes, trash, food, water. The preliminary theory is that Del Gardo was living in there, using the tunnels as a hideout."

"Could it be where he hid the treasure?"

"That's another theory," Miguel said. "We'll know more after the evidence is processed. Everybody at the lab is working overtime."

"I feel guilty for pulling you away from your work."

"No *problemo*. I'm exactly where I want to be." His voice was gentle, almost musical. "I like hanging out with a crazy, beautiful *chica*."

She felt a warm flush rising from her throat. "You wouldn't rather be at the crime lab?"

"My brother is the workaholic in the family. As for me? I'm not so intense. Life is too short to spend every minute working."

His gaze warmed her face, and she knew that she was blushing. "I agree."

"You're doing me a favor by getting me away from the crime lab. I haven't had much of a social life since I moved to Kenner City. Everything focuses on the lab." He gave Jack a final pat and stood. "And I have a project that I can do right here. Is it okay if I use your computer?"

Though she liked to keep her office sacrosanct, she couldn't refuse him anything. Scooping the baby off the floor, she also stood. "What's your project?"

"Research. I need to dig up information on the bear claw necklace we found near Aspen's car."

So much had happened that she'd almost forgotten that necklace—their first real clue. "Where do we start?"

"We'll check a couple of search engines to see if we can figure out who made the necklace and who sells similar designs. If we're lucky it'll trace to a shop that keeps receipts."

In her office, Miguel settled into her desk chair facing the computer screen. She noticed him glancing at her bookshelves where the jackets of her several Quinn Richards books stood out in brightly colored relief against her other reference books. Should she tell him her secret?

Long ago, before the first book was in print, she'd signed an agreement with her publisher not to reveal her identity. Their marketing department still thought it would hurt sales if the public knew that these action-adventure espionage books were written by a thirty-year-old virgin who lived quietly in a small town in rural Colorado. After her second book, the true identity of Quinn Richards had turned into a guessing game for critics and fans who supposed the author was a real spy for the CIA or MI6.

It wouldn't hurt to tell Miguel. She wanted to be honest with him. But she'd signed that agreement....

On the computer screen, he pulled up images of leather jewelry from this area. "I'm guessing the necklace was handmade," he said. "It's too crude to be mass produced."

She remembered the bear claw design. "It didn't look like the work of an artisan."

"Crude," he said again.

Her front doorbell rang.

Instantly, Miguel bolted from the chair. His right hand instinctively went to the holster attached to his belt. "Stay back. I'll see who it is."

Still holding Jack, she watched from the dining room while Miguel checked the small screen near the door that transmitted from the hidden camera outside. He turned back toward her. "My brother."

She moved forward as Miguel deactivated the security alarms and opened the door for his twin. As Dylan stalked into her house, she decided that he'd make a very good hero in an espionage novel. He had an intensity, an aura of danger.

In her opinion, his attitude was off-putting. She much preferred a man like Miguel who was intelligent and quietly courageous.

Dylan wasted no time with greetings or friendliness. He strode into her house and announced, "They have an ID on the dead man. It's Vincent Del Gardo."

# Chapter Twelve

Del Gardo? Emma couldn't believe it. Her bald ghost with a penchant for gold coins was Del Gardo? She'd come to think of that ghost as a friendly presence. Her opinion of Del Gardo was the opposite. He was an escaped felon, a sleazy casino owner, the primary suspect in the murder of Julie Grainger.

She looked to Dylan. "He can't be Del Gardo. Callie didn't recognize him from the sketch."

"The shaved head, beard and glasses were a disguise," he muttered. "If anybody who knew Del Gardo had gotten close to the bald guy, they would've seen right through it."

"Now we know why he threatened Callie," Miguel said. "She testified against him."

"But the ghost was helping our investigation," Emma said. "He pointed us toward Griffin's house."

"After he was dead, he didn't care if we found his hideout. He must have been trying to get there when he was shot." Miguel turned to his brother. "Knowing his identity narrows the field of suspects. Boyd Perkins was after him."

"So were dozens of other people from Vegas. By the time Del Gardo went on the run, he had a lot of enemies."

"Bridger?"

"I don't care if we find the killer." Dylan flung himself

onto the sofa. "I wanted to apprehend Del Gardo, to make him pay for Julie's death. Now, we'll never know why he killed her."

"Maybe he didn't," Emma piped up.

Both twins turned toward her. Miguel's expression was curious. Dylan exuded angry frustration.

Oblivious to the tension in the room, Jack wiggled in her arms. It was getting close to time for his bedtime feeding.

She continued, "I never knew Del Gardo in life. But when I saw him, I didn't get a negative feeling. He didn't seem like a murderer. Are you sure he killed Julie?"

"Not a hundred percent. The investigation isn't over," Dylan conceded. "We need to locate Boyd Perkins."

Miguel sat beside his twin on the sofa. "There's something I need to tell you."

Dylan rubbed his forehead. "Now what?"

"At Griffin's house, when Emma was telling us where to look, she was being directed by a ghost. It was Julie."

Dylan's eyes squeezed shut as if in physical pain. "She was there? Her spirit was there?"

"She had a message for you," Miguel said. "She doesn't want you to grieve. You should remember the good times."

"That's Julie, all right." His voice cracked. "She was always thinking about other people."

The depth of his emotions caused Emma to wonder if Julie was more than a friend. "I'm sorry, Dylan. I know this is hard. Julie wanted you to know that she's all right. Beyond pain, beyond sorrow."

He leaned forward, elbows resting on his knees. His head drooped. "I don't suppose she mentioned who killed her."

"I'm afraid not."

"If you see her again, tell her that I'll find the bastard who took her life. Tell her that I miss hearing her laugh and the way she talked textbook Spanish." He looked heavenward. *"Via con dios, mi amiga."*

She wished she could comfort him, but his steely demeanor had already fallen back into place. Showing vulnerability wasn't his way. He hauled himself off the sofa, straightened his shoulders and went to the door. "I'll see you both tomorrow."

"Take care, *vato.*"

"You, too."

Miguel locked up behind his brother and activated the security system. When he came back into the room, Emma asked, "Were Julie and your brother more than just friends?"

"Not as far as I know, but my brother doesn't talk much about the women he dates. I had a feeling, about a year ago, that there was someone special. But it didn't work out." He came closer to her. "I knew it would hurt him to be reminded of Julie, but we had to tell him."

"Julie wanted him to know."

"Her words are a good reminder. Death isn't the worst thing that can happen to a person." He gazed down into the baby's small face. "Sometimes, it's harder for the people left behind."

"If you're hinting that I should accept the idea that Jack's mother is dead, forget it."

"Aspen has been missing for over a month," he gently reminded her. "The odds are—"

"No." She refused to entertain any doubt. "If Aspen had died, I'd know. There would have been a sign. She'd come here to see her baby. She loved Jack."

"A heartfelt sentiment, but not proof."

"It's enough for me," she said.

"Me, too." A slow grin stretched his mouth. "If anybody had told me last week that I'd accept your visions as fact, I would have said they were out of their mind."

"But now you know better."

"I do." He winked. "If we're going to find your cousin, we better get back to work on that clue. The bear claw necklace."

She followed him into her office, where he sat at her computer and started scanning through Web sites for jewelry makers in Colorado and in Las Vegas. His process didn't seem much different than her own research when writing her books—gliding through various search engines and making inquiries in chat rooms.

Leaving Miguel at the computer, she took care of Jack's last feeding for the day. The baby was tired; he barely finished his bottle of formula before falling sound asleep. After she tucked him into the crib in her bedroom, she went back to the office.

Miguel looked up as she came into the room. "I found something. There's a guy on the rez who sells leather necklaces similar to the one we found. His name is Jerry Burch."

"I know him," she said, remembering a skinny kid with shaggy hair who always had a comic book sticking out of his back pocket. "He called himself The Burch, and he used to draw pictures of superheroes. I think he was a couple of years older than me and Aspen."

"So he knew your cousin," Miguel said. "Did they ever date?"

"I don't think so." In her head, she tried to picture her beautiful, vivacious cousin getting together with weird, skinny Jerry Burch. "He's not her type."

"Maybe he didn't know that. Maybe he had a crush on her."

"Like a stalker?"

"There's one way to find out. We'll take a trip to the rez tomorrow and ask around."

Because of her ghostly connections to Julie and Del Gardo, Emma hadn't thought that Aspen's attacker might be someone she knew. Though none of Aspen's friends had mentioned that she was dating somebody from the rez, they had to consider that possibility. "If Jerry Burch is Jack's father, Aspen would have told me. Besides, the timing is wrong. She got pregnant while she was in Vegas."

"Burch could have gone to Vegas to see her."

"But there's no reason to keep his identity a secret," Emma said firmly.

"Unless he's married," he suggested.

"Even it that's true—and I don't think it is—Aspen would have confided in me that her lover was a married man." In her only conversation with her cousin about Jack's father, Aspen said he was strong and brave. A good man. "She told me that she never expected to see Jack's father again. So he can't be somebody who lives on the rez."

"You think Jack's father is someone who comes from a different world than your cousin?"

She nodded. "An unlikely attraction."

"Those things happen," Miguel said.

When she looked into his face, her breath caught on a sigh. Her thoughts shifted from Aspen to herself and her own unlikely attraction to Miguel.

The house seemed extra-quiet with Jack asleep in his crib. There was only Miguel. Nothing stood between them. Unspoken questions rushed through her mind. What should she say to him? Should she kiss him again? Should she invite him into her bed? *Am I crazy?*

Tearing her gaze away from him, she took a step backward. She'd only known Miguel for a few days. Though she wanted to believe that love could strike as quickly and unexpectedly as lightning on a summer day, that wasn't the way she had lived her life. Emma was a careful woman. Her heart had been bruised too many times.

"G-g-good night," she stammered. "Sleep well."

"You, too."

Moments later, she slipped between the covers. Within seconds, she was sweating. Unaccustomed sensations raced through her. Her skin tingled. God, she was hot. She plucked at her cotton nightie, threw off the comforter. Making love to Miguel, losing her virginity to him, couldn't be a smart move.

Different worlds, they came from different worlds. Though he had learned to accept the validity of her visions, her ability still made him uncomfortable. He was a scientist, a man who relied on facts and logical deductions. Beyond that, she really didn't know anything about him. They hadn't spoken about his family. He hadn't told her the secrets connected to the Chimayo medallion. Not to mention her own big secret—her virginity.

Would he be freaked out? Would he think she was strange? She hadn't planned on being a thirty-year-old virgin; her sexual inexperience didn't signify any sort of ethical stance or need to be pure. It just happened.

If they never made love, she'd never have to tell him. It wasn't as if she had the word *virgin* tattooed on her butt. But she wanted him, wanted Miguel to be the man she remembered forever as her first time.

She rolled to her back and stared up at the ceiling, inhaling and exhaling slowly, willing her muscles to relax. Her eyes blinked closed as the knots of sexual tension gradually loosened. She ought to be able to sleep after the strenuous day she'd had. Quite a day—she'd been accosted by Bridger in her kitchen, gone for a wild ride on a motorcycle, followed a ghost to a mobster's hideout and discovered a dead body. Enough to make anybody tired. Smiling to herself, she thought of Miguel and hoped for pleasant dreams.

Slumber came quickly. No ghosts interrupted her sleep. Instead, she dreamed herself into Miguel's arms while he kissed her forehead, her eyelids and her lips. Downy softness swirled around them. She felt his embrace. At the same time, she watched herself and Miguel. They were beautiful together. He was bare-chested and bronzed. She wore a long velvet gown, scarlet. Her hair glistened, and her lips were glossy. She was the star of her own personal dream movie. Effortlessly, Miguel lifted her off her feet. Still kissing. He told her she was his *chica,* his *loca bonita. Te quiero,* I love you. His voice resonated through her, more musical than Mozart.

Her eyes opened. She was awake. Her dream vanished like the pop of a fragile soap bubble.

The digital clock beside her bed read 3:37. Almost time for Jack to be waking up. She yawned, stretched and climbed out of bed.

The light from the hallway provided enough illumination for her to walk the few steps to the crib. She looked down. Jack was gone.

Last night, Miguel had fed the baby. But two nights in a row? Too good to be true. Barefoot, she padded from her bedroom into the hall and peeked into the front room.

Miguel sat in the rocking chair with Jack on his lap. As he fed the baby a bottle, his eyelids drooped. His baggy flannel pajama bottoms puddled on the floor around his bare feet.

Bemused, she watched. This was reality. Instead of a bronzed chest and flashing emerald eyes, he had stubble on his chin and a faded gray T-shirt. The odd thing was she liked this disheveled, unkempt version of Miguel much better. She decided there was nothing sexier than a man who was willing to change diapers and get up for the middle-of-the-night feeding.

Flesh and blood, Miguel made her heart beat faster. He was the man she wanted. Tonight.

When he looked up and saw her, he nodded. Quietly, he said, "Go back to bed. Jack's asleep again."

"I want to talk." She crept into the room and sat on the sofa where he'd made his bed. She pulled the burgundy wool blanket over her legs.

Moving Jack to his shoulder, Miguel patted the baby until he heard a healthy burp, then left the room to put Jack back into the crib.

Emma had never been more awake in her life. She crossed one leg on top of the other. Her foot started bouncing. Anticipation hummed through her. She might be on the brink of the best night of her life, certainly the most passionate. *Was she ready for this?* When she reached up, her fingers tangled in her mussed hair. *I need a hairbrush. Some mascara. Oh, my God, I've got to brush my teeth.*

Bolting off the sofa, she dashed into the bathroom. There was enough moonlight shining through the upper part of the window above the café curtains to find her toothpaste. She squeezed a glob. Her fingers were trembling. She turned on the electric toothbrush.

Miguel appeared in the mirror behind her. In the dim light, he was a shadow.

"What are you doing?" he asked.

*Making a fool of myself. Having second thoughts.* She gestured with the toothbrush. "Since I was awake, I thought—"

He turned her toward him, took the toothbrush from her hand and turned it off. "Dental hygiene can wait. What's up?"

"Apparently, you are." Moonlight slanted across his face, hiding his cheekbones.

"You're shivering, Emma."

"I'm fine." She stepped back, bumping against the tiled counter. "Thank you, Miguel. For helping me out and getting up with the baby. It means a lot to me."

*"De nada."* He glanced over his shoulders. "When you

said you wanted to talk, I thought you had a visitor. Another ghost."

"Not this time." Ignoring her nervousness, she reached toward him, rested her palm on the center of his chest, near his heart. "We're alone, Miguel. And the baby is asleep."

Just to make sure her invitation was obvious, she tilted her head upward. Her lips parted.

Leaning down, he kissed her slowly and thoroughly. Her shivers of tension transformed into a steady, throbbing pulse. Her hands climbed his chest, and she circled her arms around his neck.

His lean, muscular body pressed against her, trapping her against the countertop. Only a thin layer of clothing separated their naked flesh. She arched against him. The pressure set off a chain reaction of excitement that spread from head to toe.

He glided his hands down her side, grazing her breasts, and cupped her bottom.

Breathless, she gasped. "Miguel."

"Yes, Emma." He kissed her throat.

"There's something I should tell you." Another tremor slid through her. "Something you ought to know about me."

"It's okay. I already know."

*How could he know she was a virgin?* "What? How?"

With a devastatingly handsome smile, he gazed into her eyes. "Don't worry. Your secret is safe with me."

Her embrace loosened. "What the hell are you talking about?"

"When I was in your office." He stroked the line of her jaw. "I saw that row of books by Quinn Richards, and remembered your grandma Quinn. And your last name is Richardson. Then I looked at the photo on the book jacket— a cleverly morphed picture of you. You're Quinn Richards."

"You were spying on me." She was shocked, appalled,

hurt. Damn him. It felt like he'd thrown a bucket of ice water over her head. "How could you?"

"I'm an investigator. I look at the scene and make deductions. It really didn't seem like—"

"You had no right." She shoved him away from her. There would be no more embraces, no caresses. And, definitely, no lovemaking. "I can't trust you."

"Come on, Emma. You were secretive about your office, and I wanted to know why. I couldn't help figuring it out."

"Congratulations." She wedged out from between him and the counter. "You're much too clever for me."

Before she could leave the bathroom, he grasped her arm. "There's no problem. You were about to tell me, anyway."

"Actually, you're wrong." She slapped his hand away. "I have another secret. A much more important one. And you'll never find out what it is."

He didn't deserve to know. He'd pried into her affairs without her consent. Miguel was an untrustworthy sneak.

She'd never confide in him. It would be a cold day in hell when her sexual experience or lack thereof had anything whatsoever to do with him.

# Chapter Thirteen

The next morning as they loaded the baby supplies into the car for the trip to the Ute Mountain Ute reservation, Miguel cursed his bad timing. Last night, he'd chosen exactly the wrong moment to bring up a topic that was sure to make Emma mad—her secret identity as Quinn Richards. *Dios mio,* he was a donkey. No wonder his brother got all the *chicas.* Dylan would have known better.

But Miguel couldn't help who he was. He spoke the truth and didn't play games. However, as a scientist, he could also be patient, *muy* patient. He would wait for Emma to come around.

In the meantime, he was itching to know her other secret. He told himself to let it go, but his brain wouldn't stop chasing after the answer.

Constantly observing her, he constructed theories about her secret, ranging from unlikely espionage plots—she was a smuggler of ancient Incan artifacts—to the mundane. A tattoo? A weird birthmark?

All morning, her attitude toward him had been cool but polite. She didn't pout or give him the silent treatment, for which he was grateful. But he missed those little glances she took when she thought he wasn't looking. Her voice was no longer soft and breathy when she said his name.

Instead, she sounded like Sister Consuelo, his third-grade teacher, who used to smack his knuckles with a ruler.

As they drove east in her car toward the rez, she made a number of calls on her cell phone to friends and members of her extended family until she got a phone number and location for Jerry Burch's studio.

Emma turned to check on Jack, who had fallen asleep in the baby seat. She asked, "Should I call Jerry Burch?"

"It's better if we stop in unannounced." Standard procedure for interrogating a suspect. "If he's somehow involved in Aspen's disappearance, we don't want him to have time to come up with a pack of lies. What did you find out about him?"

"He's been divorced for a couple of years. Has two children with his ex-wife, who lives in Denver. According to Dolly Zeto—a friend of Aspen's—Jerry has a fairly successful line of custom Native American jewelry."

"Did Dolly mention a connection between Aspen and Jerry?"

"None at all. Jerry's a quiet guy who keeps to himself."

With a cynical nod, Miguel digested the brief biography. Jerry Burch sounded innocent enough—maybe too innocent. "It's the quiet ones you have to look out for."

"I thought that was a cliché." Her tone was snippy. "Like when people who live next door to psycho murderers describe them as good neighbors?"

"Most clichés are based on truth." He couldn't help giving her a dig about her secret identity. "You've probably found that to be true in your writing as Quinn Richards."

Her shoulders stiffened. She stared straight ahead through the windshield. "I will not discuss Quinn Richards. I signed an agreement with my publisher to never reveal my identity to anyone."

"Why?"

"Because the Quinn Richards books are marketed as action-packed adventures of espionage. It'd hurt sales if anyone found out that the author is a single woman living in rural Colorado."

"So you're selling the reading public a lie."

"No," she said firmly. "I could have made up an author biography about being a former CIA operative or a world adventurer. Instead, I say nothing."

"There's a phony picture of you on the book jacket."

"But it's still my picture." She glared at him. "How did you recognize me in that photo?"

"I've played around with those morphing programs enough to see through them." He met her glare. "Besides, I'd know your beautiful eyes anywhere."

He wasn't offering an idle compliment. From the first time he'd seen her, Miguel connected with that special glimmer in her eyes—a hot blue spark that lit a flame inside him.

They drove for a while without talking. The rez covered a lot of empty terrain, most of which wasn't good for farming or grazing. The major sources of income for the tribe were the casino and the pottery factory.

As they drove deeper into the rez, Emma's Ute heritage became more apparent. She had stories about powwows and spring rituals. All her directions came from landmarks. Turn east at the seven pine trees. Go south on the hogback ridge.

He pulled up at a stop sign at a crossroads. On the northeast corner was a ramshackle storefront with several hand-painted signs advertising food, beer and—oddly enough—hot espresso. "Which way?"

"East. Toward the red cliffs."

Trying to avoid the bigger potholes in the poorly paved road, he drove slowly. "I'm guessing that Jerry Burch doesn't have many people coming to visit his studio."

"Most of the local artists don't," she said. "Either they have booths at powwows or they sell on commission through established shops in the big cities or tourist destinations."

"I know how it works. *Mi madre* teaches art at Adams State."

"Does she paint?"

"Mostly, she does photography. She's been getting into computer art that's kind of amazing. It looks real and surreal at the same time. I can show you her Web site."

"I'd like that." To his surprise, her voice softened perceptively. "Do you realize that's the first thing you've told me about your family?"

"Is it?"

"You change the subject every time it turns toward you. We've been together twenty-four-seven almost since we met, and I hardly know anything about you."

"You know I play guitar," he reminded her. "And I ride a motorcycle."

"Tell me about your family."

"Five kids. Papa is a lawyer, but not the kind that makes a lot of money. He calls himself King Pro Bono. My sister and other brother are married with kids."

"A sister, brother and twins." She tallied the numbers. "That's only four."

"My sister, Teresa, died when she was fifteen." Not a topic he liked to talk about. He still missed Teresa. "She was murdered."

On the left side of the road, he saw a mailbox with Burch printed in elaborate letters. He took the turn, heading toward two small houses, side by side, both whitewashed stucco. One was two-story with a wide door like a barn.

As they approached, he heard the roar of hard-driving, heavy-metal music. "Jerry Burch isn't as quiet as your friend thought."

After he parked and Emma freed Jack from the baby seat, they approached the smaller door on the side of the tall house. The hyper-amped volume on the music sounded like a heavy-metal concert in progress.

As soon as Miguel knocked, he realized the futility of that motion. No one could hear a tap on the door over the blasting music from inside. Taking his badge from his pocket, he pushed open the door and stepped inside.

He found himself staring down the barrel of a rifle.

Quickly, he held up his badge. "Police."

A man with long black hair flying loose around his shoulders tapped a switch with his moccasin. Silence.

"Police," Miguel repeated. "I'm from the Kenner County Crime Lab."

"You got no jurisdiction on the rez, man."

Emma stepped out from behind him. "Jerry Burch?"

His eyes narrowed as he studied her. "Emma?"

"You remember me." She beamed.

He lowered the rifle. "What the hell are you doing here? Who's the baby?"

As she brushed past Miguel, she said under her breath, "Not calling ahead was a great idea."

"Maybe not," he muttered.

"Let me handle this."

He nodded. Being in the sight of a rifle reminded him that there was more going on than his issues with Emma. This was an investigation, and the danger was real.

While Emma and Jerry hugged and she introduced him to Jack, Miguel took a look around the studio. High windows flooded the one huge room with natural sunlight. A white table in one corner held a clutter of precision engraving and welding tools—apparently the area where Burch did his custom jewelry work. Every bit of wall space was hung with artwork—photographs, portraits and pop art drawings of muscular superheroes from comic books.

Burch came toward him with hand outstretched. "Sorry about the gun, man. I got a lot of silver and turquoise lying around."

Miguel shook his hand. Though Jerry Burch was nearly his height, he was as skinny as Emma had remembered. His rib cage showed through his tight, blue superhero T-shirt. "We need your help with our investigation."

The corners of his mouth pulled down. "Hey, I don't rat out my brothers."

"It's about Aspen," Emma said. "To help find Aspen."

He immediately changed his mind. "Then I'll help. Hell, yeah. What can I do?"

Miguel reached into his jacket pocket and produced a photograph of the bear claw necklace. "What can you tell me about this?"

"Man, I did a bunch of these. Maybe a hundred. Handmade. I burned the image into the leather."

"Uh-huh." Miguel didn't care about the artistic process unless it included a GPS chip to locate the wearer of the necklace. "All bear claws?"

"Different images." He ran his hand through his long hair. "Hawk. Howling coyote. Turtle."

"How many were bear claws?"

"Geez, I don't know. Maybe twenty or thirty. It was a while back. Maybe seven years ago. I'm a better artist now." He turned toward Emma. "Want to see some of my stuff?"

"You bet." She followed him to the worktable.

Miguel didn't want to waste time looking at squash blossom necklaces and concha belts. "I have more questions."

Emma whirled toward him. "Not yet, Miguel. This is how we do things on the rez. We take our time. We socialize."

"She's right." Burch laughed. "Slow and easy. That's why Utes are good lovers."

"Relax," she told him. "Allow the string to unwind."

He adjusted his thinking to her culture, which wasn't so different from his own. As a kid, he'd spent hours listening to the old ones tell stories that circled and looped and came back around to the beginning. Sometimes, there was a point. Other times, not.

Burch's jewelry didn't follow the traditional patterns. Instead, he incorporated Ute designs in braided strands of thin wire and dramatic pendants that showed some of his comic book influence. "You like superheroes," Miguel said.

"Ever since I was a kid and I found Indian superheroes in the comics. I wanted to be like them." He gestured toward a life-size painting. "That's my own creation. Pinto Hawk. He rides like the wind and flies like a bird, wreaking vengeance on evil-doers."

Miguel picked up his thread. "Evil-doers like the man who made Aspen disappear."

"Let me see that picture of the bear claw again." Burch studied his own handiwork. "Most of these were sold through a shop in Durango and here on the rez by a guy who went out of business and moved on."

Tracing the sale through old receipts would be a dead end. Miguel asked, "Who would still be wearing the bear claw seven years later?"

"Somebody who thought the claw brought him luck. Or protected him. You know, like a totem." His dark eyes— nearly black—scanned up and to the right, as if looking for a memory. "There was one guy who lived on the rez. Scuzzy. Kind of mean-looking. I noticed him because I thought it was cool that he was wearing something I made."

"Do you remember his name?"

"Not sure I ever knew it." He darted across the room,

moving silently on his moccasins, and pointed to a photograph. "There. The guy in the flat-brim hat."

The picture showed three men loitering on a wood slat porch. The bear claw was clearly visible, but the face of the man wearing the necklace was in shadow.

"That's him," Emma said.

"You can't see his features," Miguel said.

"Do you see the knife on his belt?" Her blue eyes pierced through him. "That's the man who attacked my cousin."

EMMA HAD SEEN THE faceless man in her vision. He'd been chasing her, trying to kill her with his knife. And she was fairly sure that he was the same man who'd broken into her house and disabled her car. A shadow man.

When they found him, she knew he'd lead them to Aspen.

Tracking down his name was going to take time. "If we showed this picture to somebody at the tribal newspaper, maybe they could identify him."

"Lydia Fife," Burch said. "That lady knows everybody and their ancestors."

"I guess we need to go there." She started the bouncy walk that usually calmed the baby. "It's not really that far. Only about half an hour."

Miguel turned to Burch. "You got a fax machine?"

"Sure thing, man. I'm in business."

In his quiet way, Miguel took control of the situation. He lifted Jack from her arms. "What's your problem, *mijo?* You come with me. Emma, contact the newspaper and get a name for this guy."

"Good plan."

"And you might want to tell her to keep it quiet."

As if that would happen. As soon as they started making inquiries, everybody would know. Gossip on the rez spread fast and wide, like seeds on the wind.

While Miguel fed Jack his bottle and got him quieted down, she and Burch contacted the newspaper office via phone and then by fax. Though it seemed to her that minutes were ticking by like hours, Lydia Fife was able to identify the man with the bear claw necklace.

Before she bid farewell to Burch, she bought a pendant. It had been good to renew their acquaintance, and she sincerely wished him well.

"Sherman Watts." Emma repeated the name as she and Miguel returned to her car. "I recognized the flat-brimmed hat. He was the one who messed with my car."

"Not Boyd Perkins?"

She shook her head. "Watts is the guy. Let's get him."

"Whoa, *chica*. Much as I'd like to make an arrest before he knows we're after him, that's not my job."

"You have a gun," she said. "And a badge."

"Which means nothing on the rez." Carrying the baby, he circled to the passenger side. "You drive. I'll make some phone calls."

"Where are we going?"

"To your house. Where it's safe." He got Jack situated in his baby seat. "We can't chase after the bad guys while *mijo* is with us."

He had a point. Emma was usually cautious to the point of meekness, but her blood was boiling. In her action-adventure novels, she often wrote about men and women engaged in life-and-death struggles. They were brave and proactive. They were steely-eyed predators. Right now, she knew how that felt. Her skin tingled. Adrenaline raced through her veins. She felt the urge to rush forward, no matter what the danger.

Slipping behind the wheel, she scooted the seat forward, fastened her seat belt and adjusted the rearview mirror. "Oh, swell."

"What is it?" Miguel asked.

Her head swiveled as she peered into the backseat. The ghost of Aunt Rose was sitting beside Jack. It made sense that she'd be here on the rez where she'd spent most of her life. Unsmiling, she said, "You be careful, Emma. Sherman Watts is a bad person. Mean in spirit. His heart is stone."

"I know."

Miguel's eyes narrowed. "Another ghost."

"My aunt Rose."

In a low voice, Aunt Rose continued, "Sherman Watts isn't the only danger. Watch out for the Vegas cowboy."

"What else can you tell me?"

"Don't use a pacifier with the baby. It makes his teeth strange."

In a poof, she was gone. Emma muttered under her breath, "Sometimes, I wish my friendly spirit guides would be a little more specific."

"Is she gone?"

"Oh, yeah." She cranked the key in the ignition and headed to her house.

Though the dire warning from Aunt Rose had lessened Emma's desire to strap on a gun and lead the assault team that would track down Sherman Watts, she was still buzzed. They'd had a very productive morning. They'd found the name of the bastard who attacked Aspen. Sherman Watts.

As she drove west, taking the shortest route to Kenner City, she heard Miguel repeat that name several times as he made calls on his cell phone. Who was he talking to? What was the plan? Even though she wasn't technically part of law enforcement, she'd earned the right to know what was going on.

His conversation stopped abruptly. Staring at the phone, he poked the buttons. "No reception."

"There are a lot of places around here that don't get cell-phone reception."

"I guess you'd know all about dead zones. Being a medium."

She was too pleased with herself to be irritated by his teasing. "Very funny. Laughing on the inside."

Miguel turned in his seat so he was facing the back window of the car as he said, "The lab turned up a couple of leads on Del Gardo's murder. Ballistics tests show the bullet to be .45 caliber from a Sig Sauer. No match on file."

She prompted, "Which means?"

"It wasn't from the gun previously used by Boyd Perkins," Miguel said. "But that doesn't take him off the list of suspects. He could have a new gun."

"What else?"

"This is interesting." He played with Jack, eliciting giggles from the baby. "Remember the map with the VDG symbol? The map Julie sent?"

"Of course."

"Those twists and turns seem to match up with the tunnels under Griffin's house. Julie must have gone through those caves. There's something down there she wanted us to find."

"I think we already found it," she said. "Del Gardo himself."

"You're probably right. She mapped the tunnels in case Del Gardo decided to use his hideout. Unfortunately, by the time he was holed up in the tunnels, Julie was already dead."

"Killed by Del Gardo," Emma said. "Supposedly."

"The map is another clue pointing in that direction. Julie was onto him. He had to take her out."

"I still don't believe it." Del Gardo's ghost seemed more like Santa Claus than a bloodthirsty killer. "There's one thing I still don't understand. With all those millions of dollars, why was he hanging around in cold, dark tunnels outside Kenner City?"

"There was something here he wanted. Revenge on Callie, maybe. Or this might be the place where he hid his treasure. Ava and Bobby are going through the tunnels inch by inch looking for signs that something was in there and moved."

"That's possible. The first time I saw Del Gardo's ghost, he was digging up gold coins. Maybe I'm supposed to interpret that to mean that he'd moved the treasure."

Miguel continued to look over his shoulder. "I don't want you to panic, Emma. But I think we're being followed."

# Chapter Fourteen

Emma's leg jolted in a reflex action. She pressed down harder on the accelerator, and her car jumped forward like a jackrabbit. *Being followed?* They were in the middle of nowhere—a literal dead zone. "What should I do?"

"He's a good distance back, over half a mile. I can just make out the glint of sunlight on his car."

"If I went faster, I could lose him."

"That's a plan," he said diplomatically. "But there's only one road—this road—leading off the rez. That's why he can stay so far back. He knows where we're going."

"I could take a turnoff." As soon as she spoke, she realized that escape route was iffy. "But it might lead to a dead end. Then we'd be trapped."

His hand lightly stroked her arm. Instead of jerking away and avoiding him, she appreciated the physical contact. No matter how irritated she was with him, Miguel always made her feel safe.

"Here's what we do," he said. "I'll keep an eye on the other car. If he's still following us when we get closer to Kenner City, I'll call Sheriff Martinez for support."

"Who would be following us?"

"Maybe Bridger." He squinted as he peered through the

back window. "Wish I could identify his vehicle. I don't suppose you have binoculars in your car."

"Sorry, I don't generally carry long-range surveillance equipment," she said. "If we were in need of baby wipes, I'd be well supplied."

When she heard him chuckle, her hands almost slipped off the wheel. Was he actually laughing? On the outside? In spite of her stated goal to curtail their relationship, it seemed to be growing of its own accord—like a weed in a garden of roses.

His cell phone rang, and he answered.

Though she checked her rearview mirrors frequently, she only caught faraway glimpses of the car that appeared to be tailing them.

"That was Dylan," Miguel said as he disconnected the call. "There's a jurisdictional problem. The FBI can't arrest Sherman Watts while he's on the reservation. And Sheriff Martinez can't make arrests on the rez, either."

"What about Patrick's fiancée, Bree Hunter? She's a Ute cop," Emma said. "Surely, she can take Watts into custody."

"Dylan talked to Bree. She's not real impressed with our evidence. All we have to link Watts to Aspen's disappearance is the necklace."

"And my vision." Emma knew that testimony from a medium didn't count for much. "Can't the crime lab come up with something more? Like DNA on the necklace? I've read about touch DNA."

He groaned. "So has everybody else. Technically, it's possible to make a DNA identification from a minuscule amount—only a few cells left behind when someone touches an object."

"Right," she said. "They can get DNA from a fingerprint."

"Why bother? A fingerprint ought to be identification enough. It's a painstaking laboratory process to extract those cells for DNA analysis. It could take weeks."

"According to the literature on the subject, touch DNA—"

"Is this research for a Quinn Richards book?"

At the mention of her pseudonym, her jaw clenched. Why had he brought it up? She didn't want to be angry with him. "As I told you before, discussion of my work is off-limits. I won't talk about it."

"I respect your decision," he said. "There's only one thing I have to say, then *silencio*. I'll shut up forever."

There wasn't anything she could do to stop him from making a comment. Since they were being tailed by a bad guy, she couldn't pull over to the side of the road and order Miguel to get out of the car. "Fine."

"I started reading one of your books last night. It was good, really good. I'm proud of you, Emma."

His unexpected statement disarmed her. For the past five years, she'd been writing books that sold very well and were critically acclaimed. Though she took satisfaction from glowing reviews, she'd never been in the spotlight. "Proud?"

"You've got talent. And smarts, too. You're writing about a world you don't know much about."

"I've always been good at research." His praise warmed her. "And my copy editor is good at catching errors."

"You're the one who does the hard part, the writing part. You deserve an Academy Award."

"They don't give Oscars for books, silly." Her hostility toward him began to ebb. "Actually, Quinn Richards has won a couple of prizes. My editor picked them up for me."

"Next time, you should be there to hear the applause."

He sounded sincere; his voice lacked the edge of cynicism that signaled his teasing. But she found his compliments difficult to accept. Throughout her life, she'd never expected others to support her goals, to praise her or be proud.

When she gazed into his green eyes, she knew he was

telling the truth. He honestly admired her accomplishments. "I don't know what to say."

"It's simple, *querida*. Say thank you."

Tenderness washed through her. No way could she hold a grudge against him. "*Gracias,* Miguel."

"*De nada.*" He looked through the back window again. "I think it's a black SUV."

"Bridger," she said. "Is he getting closer?"

"Don't worry," Miguel said. "We're almost at the turn leading toward Kenner City. I can call for backup."

Tension tightened her shoulders. She had no desire to get into a chase, certainly not with Jack in the car. Long, desolate miles stretched ahead of them.

While Miguel made more phone calls, she imagined a hawk's-eye view of the road. Looking down from the skies, her car and the SUV following them would be as small as ants crawling along a mountain pass—separate but on the same trail, a ribbon of road leading to an uncertain future.

At the stop sign, she turned left.

As she proceeded, still following the speed limit, Miguel continued to stare through the rear window. "He went right."

Relieved, Emma exhaled in a whoosh. "He wasn't following us after all."

"Maybe not." Miguel didn't sound convinced. "But it was a black SUV, like Bridger's vehicle."

"We should call Sheriff Martinez. He could—"

"By the time he got anywhere near here, the SUV would be long gone," Miguel said. "For now, we need to concentrate on Sherman Watts."

Logically, she knew he was right. Intuitively, she felt a greater threat from Sherman Watts—a shadow man who threatened her in a vision. But the continued presence of Bridger worried her. He was after a treasure—millions of dollars—and wouldn't quit until he found it.

When they finally got to her house, it was after two o'clock. Jack was awake and wiggling. She lifted him from the car seat. "You've been such a good boy."

He waved his little arms like he was directing an invisible orchestra. And he smiled.

"Good baby," she repeated.

He'd put up with a lot of disruption to his schedule. And so had she. All this crime-solving was exhausting, and she was longing to relax for the rest of the day. Then, maybe, spend a quiet evening with Miguel. After dinner, they might take up where they left off last night.

She'd more than forgiven him for prying into her secret identity as Quinn Richards. As he'd said, he couldn't stop himself from figuring it out.

At the front door, she paused, waiting while Miguel went into the house first and disconnected the security alarm.

Emma turned toward the street.

A black SUV rolled slowly by. Through the open window, she saw Hank Bridger. He grinned at her and gave a wave before driving on.

A FEW HOURS LATER, Emma emerged from the bedroom after putting Jack to sleep. The afternoon had segued into dusk. She sprawled on the sofa and looked toward Miguel who sat in the rocking chair with his cell phone within easy reach.

Though his eyelids drooped at half-mast, he didn't look as tired as he should have been. His first call had been to the sheriff, who had considered putting up roadblocks to catch Bridger. Then, Miguel was in constant communication with the crime lab and with his brother. For the past couple of hours, Miguel had been talking nonstop.

Even so, his steady gaze held a glimmer of energy. A steady flame like a pilot light. She had no doubt that, if encouraged, he could rise from the rocker and sweep her off her feet.

Now might be the perfect time. Her resistance was low, and she was oh-so-ready to be held and cherished. And make love?

She exhaled a sigh, amazed that she could contemplate such an earth-shaking, life-changing event. She cleared her throat. "How did you get to be at the center of all these phone calls?"

"I work at the lab. Normally, I wouldn't have much to do with the FBI, but Dylan is my twin brother—which gives people the mistaken idea that I have some influence over him." He shook his head. "And Sheriff Martinez is my friend."

"Any word from the sheriff? Did he find Bridger?"

"Not yet."

"If they do locate him, can they arrest him?"

"You bet." He cocked his head to one side. "What makes you think otherwise?"

"When we looked him up, he had no outstanding warrants. And he's gotten off on every crime he's been charged with."

"He broke into your house, Emma. That's enough for an arrest. Also, he's a person of interest in the Del Gardo murder."

"But Bridger didn't want Del Gardo dead. All he's interested in is the money." Stretching her legs straight out in front of her, she kicked off her purple sneakers and wiggled her toes. "It doesn't make sense that he'd kill Del Gardo."

"Motives aren't my problem. My job is finding the facts and analyzing them." He steepled his fingers and peered at her over the arch. "So far, we have one good piece of evidence that could point to Bridger."

"What's that?"

"The boot print we found at the crime scene. A size thirteen. The shape is distinctive. It's probably custom-made footwear."

"And Bridger is a snappy dresser. I think his boots were snakeskin."

The cell phone on the table beside him rang. He picked it up and glared at the caller ID. "It's the lab again."

"Go ahead and take it." She pushed herself off the sofa. "I'm going to check my e-mail."

After grabbing a bottle of water from the fridge, she went into the office and turned on the computer. There was an e-mail from her editor asking how she was doing on her latest novel. If Emma could turn it in early, the editor would like to move the pub date up.

In the past, such a request would have thrown her into a tizzy. But now? It was nothing. *Nada.* Emma's life had changed since that moment when she sat at this very desk and had the vision that set her on the path to finding Aspen. Because of that vision, she'd met Miguel. And since she'd met him, many of her priorities had shifted.

The phone on her desk rang, and she picked up.

"Hello, Miss Emma."

"Bridger." She bolted upright in her chair.

"So glad you recognize my voice," he said smoothly.

As if she would ever forget? Talking to him was like sticking her finger into an electric socket. "Why were you following me?"

"You know what I'm looking for. And I've heard tell that there's some kind of treasure map. True?"

She remembered the map Julie had drawn that outlined the twists and turns of the tunnels under Griffin's house. "True."

"I'd sure like to get my hands on that map," he said. "And I think you can help me. I have a proposition for you, Miss Emma."

Common sense told her to hang up; never make a deal with the devil. Still, she asked, "What's in it for me?"

"I have information about the disappearance of your cousin."

She'd be a fool to trust him. But there might be a kernel of truth in what he said. She picked up a pen and held it poised above a clean sheet of paper, ready to write down whatever he said. "Go on."

"Not so fast. We're playing a little game here. You tell me something. Then I tell you."

Her vision went fuzzy around the edges—similar to the way she felt before succumbing to a vision. *Not now. Oh, God. Not now.* She needed to be alert.

"The map," she said. "It starts near three pine trees up on a hill and a marking on a rock that looks like a crescent moon."

"Where do I find these trees?"

"Tit for tat," she said. "You have to tell me something first."

He made a sound that could have been a laugh or a snarl. "You'd make a decent poker player, Miss Emma. With that sweet pink mouth and big blue eyes, you look real innocent. But you're sharp."

On the other side of the office near the bookcase, she saw a shape begin to form. Then another. She needed to talk fast. "Mr. Bridger, you said you had information."

"That's right." His voice dropped even lower. It sounded like he was talking from the bottom of a well.

"Well." The word echoed around her. "Well?"

"Sherman Watts wasn't acting alone."

"Who was he working with?"

"Your turn, Miss Emma."

She figured she'd string him along with a description of the entrance to the tunnel without revealing too much. She'd talk about a cold, dark place and mention a map that had fooled the FBI and the crime lab.

But the atmosphere in her office had transformed. A chill seeped into her bones. The ethereal shapes became more substantial. A dark man and a pretty woman with blond ringlets stood in front of her bookcase.

They were both connected to Bridger.

"Miss Emma," he said. "Don't try my patience."

The sound of his voice gave them life. As the woman came closer, Emma saw the hard lines in her face. Her lipstick was bloodred. "He killed me."

"And me," said the man. He paced back and forth with a limp. "Killed me dead."

"Mr. Bridger…"

The irony of her predicament hit her. When she saw him before, she'd pretended to see the victims of his crimes. Now, they were here. A man and woman. And someone else. A third presence was forming.

Emma looked down at her desk. Though she was unaware of writing anything, two names were clearly spelled out. She read them aloud. "Simone Caparelli. Burton Nestor."

"What the hell are you talking about?"

"You know what I'm saying." She stared at the bookshelf. The third presence took shape. Another man.

"You can't prove a damn thing," he said. "Don't try to threaten me."

She looked into the bearded face of the familiar ghost. His smile was sad.

"You killed Vincent Del Gardo," she said. "He's here. I can see him."

As if from faraway, she heard Bridger say, "You'll be joining Del Gardo. Soon."

The telephone receiver slipped from her hand. She might have hung up. Not sure.

Her vision darkened as her head dropped forward. When

she looked up, the walls of her office had disappeared. Del Gardo held out his hand in a courtly gesture.

She rose to her feet. Accompanied by the ghosts of three murder victims, she stepped into a vision.

## Chapter Fifteen

Entering a world beyond reality, Emma strolled across flagstones toward a nighttime fiesta with bright lights strung from the branches of trees. Women in flowing, colorful skirts twirled and clapped in time to lively mariachi music. Even though she knew this was a vision, she found herself searching the faces of the men, looking for Miguel.

"Keep moving," Del Gardo said.

She looked over at his shiny, bald head. "When I first saw you, why didn't you tell me who you were?"

"I had other things on my mind." He scowled. "Like being dead."

She couldn't argue with that logic; death was a difficult transition. Walking abreast, they passed adobe-colored storefronts and crossed a street to enter a town square filled with huge earthenware pots of azaleas, purple pansies and yellow petunias.

In the brightly lit gazebo, the mariachi band played. Four men in sombreros thumped their guitars. Another fingered his accordion. The lead singer, gesturing with his coronet, hit a high tenor note, looking like he might burst right out of his tight black pants with silver buttons down the side.

The blond woman, Simone, took the hand of the limping

man. They danced away together, leaving Emma with Del Gardo, who still scowled, showing no sign of pleasure amid these festive sights and sounds.

"What's wrong?" she asked.

"Others will die."

"Who?"

"And I have no way to stop the murder."

From everything she'd been told about Del Gardo, he was mired in crime—a truly evil person. But that wasn't her impression. His distress about the murders seemed utterly sincere.

"Will my cousin die?" She had so many questions. Bridger had said that Sherman Watts hadn't been working alone. Who was his partner? Where was he? "What else can you tell me?"

Del Gardo took a step away from her.

"Wait," she called after him. Emma knew better than to press for answers to specific questions. Her visions weren't meant to predict the future. She might see future influences, but the spirits never offered specifics.

When Del Gardo turned back toward her, he was wearing a grin and a huge sombrero. Looking down, Emma saw that her outfit had changed. She wore a full skirt of purple with white stars. Though not aware of dancing, her skirt swished back and forth in time to the music.

Del Gardo touched her hand and led her into the throng.

"I'm trying to understand," she said. "What do you want me to see?"

He doffed his Mexican hat and bowed low.

Her feet started moving. She didn't know the steps, but she was dancing, fitting in very nicely with all the other fiesta-goers in the square. As they stomped and twirled, she wished Miguel could see her.

A dark *vaquero* took her hand and spun her in a graceful

circle. He was handsome but no match for Miguel. When she pulled away from him, another man took his place.

"No, no," she protested. "I don't have time to dance."

They laughed…too loudly, slightly maniacal. She didn't want to be dancing when there was so much else to be done. She had to find Aspen.

But the dancing men wouldn't let her stop, wouldn't let her catch her breath. Swirling and dipping and clicking their heels, an endless string of partners yanked her into the center of the dancers. Her shoulders hurt from being pulled in too many directions.

"Excuse me," she shouted. "I have to go."

The thrumming music got louder. The voices of the mariachis howled.

At the edge of the circle, she spotted Del Gardo and his two companions. Their faces were cold. Somber.

She tried to run, but the circle closed more tightly around her. The women rustled their skirts and made yipping noises.

Then she saw Bridger. His fringe on his garish jacket jostled with every step. The snakeskin band on his hat came to life, hissing and rattling. His large hands dripped blood.

She tried to run, but couldn't escape from the circle. A wall of laughing dancers blocked her way.

There was a loud popping noise. Fireworks. All the dancers threw their hats into the air. Dozens of sombreros soared high in the night sky.

Slowly, slowly, they fell.

When they touched the ground, the fiesta was gone.

The night became so utterly silent that she could hear the rapid beating of her own heart. She sat at the desk in her office, staring at the bookcase.

"Emma?" Miguel stepped into the office. "Are you okay?"

She held out her arms, and he drew her from the chair into an embrace.

AFTER A JUMBLED EXPLANATION, Miguel got Emma settled at the kitchen table. He ignored the constant ring tone of his cell phone and concentrated only on her. This vision had taken a lot out of her. She gazed up at him with frightened eyes. "A party doesn't sound terrible, but it was. They wouldn't let me stop dancing. The music was so loud."

"Mariachi music," he said.

"What does it mean?" Tension pinched the corners of her mouth. "Del Gardo showed me the fiesta for a reason, but I can't for the life of me figure it out."

"And the two names you wrote down?"

"That part is clear," she said. "Simone and Burton. They told me that Bridger killed them. And Del Gardo, too."

"And you mentioned these names to Bridger."

"I think so. Things were getting hazy at that point."

This was not good. By telling Bridger that she knew the identities of his victims, Emma put herself at greater risk. If the Vegas cowboy believed she could link him to past crimes, she became a threat. His casual surveillance— following her car from a couple hundred yards away—might get a hell of a lot more personal.

In spite of the security system at her house, Miguel wasn't sure he could protect her from a determined killer. "I think I need more backup tonight."

"Whatever is necessary." She leaned forward, elbows on the table, and rubbed at her forehead. "I wish I could figure out that vision."

"Tell me the details."

She described a town square with azaleas and dancers in bright colors. "My skirt was purple," she said.

"Your favorite color."

"I looked for you in the crowd, but you weren't there."

"Too bad." He gave her an encouraging smile. "I'd like to see you dance."

"In my vision, I was graceful. In real life, I've got two left feet." As if to show him, she staggered to her feet. "I'm thirsty. I should have some water."

"Sit." He touched her shoulder, and she obeyed—too tired to protest. He said, "I was thinking of something stronger than water."

"There's a bottle of wine in the back of the cabinet by the door."

After a quick search, he found a dusty bottle of burgundy. While he dug through drawers, looking for a corkscrew, he asked, "What other details do you remember? How about the music itself? What were they playing?"

"I'm not sure. There was that song that goes like this: Dum-dee-dee-dum-dum. De-dum."

He winced. It was the most tuneless rendering he'd ever heard. Musicality wasn't one of her talents. "Try it again."

"You know what I'm talking about." She went through her humming again, then clapped her hands twice. "Dum-dee-dee-dum-dum. De-dum. Clap, clap. It's the Mexican Hat Dance."

A favorite of grade-school teachers. He opened the wine and poured a glass for her and for himself. "Does that song have any particular meaning for you?"

"I don't know the words." She accepted the wine. "Isn't it something like, dance with your partner, olé?"

"Something like that."

"They all threw their sombreros in the air," she said. "And the mariachis did that song with the dramatic guitar and the high tenor."

"Don't try to sing it." He clinked his wineglass with hers and took a sip. "We'll talk about music later."

Taking out his cell phone, he stepped into the dining

room and speed dialed Sheriff Martinez. After quickly
filling him in on the broad outline of Emma's vision, he
added two requests. The first was for dinner.

"Fine," Martinez said. "I'll grab something from
Mama's café."

"Also, on your way over here, can you stop at my place
and pick up my guitar? There's a musical piece of evidence
we need to work through."

"Sure." The sheriff paused. "Have you heard from
your brother?"

"Only about a thousand times today."

"Recently?"

Miguel thought for a moment. "Maybe an hour ago.
Maybe more. Why?"

"I hope he doesn't do something stupid."

Sheriff Martinez didn't need to go into details. Miguel
knew how frustrated Dylan was with the slow process of
arranging for the arrest of Sherman Watts on the reservation. *Dios mio,* they were all frustrated. But Dylan had the
resources of the FBI behind him if he decided to make an
abrupt move.

"When Emma talked to Bridger," Miguel said, "he told
her that Watts wasn't acting alone."

"Doesn't surprise me. Watts is no mastermind. He's a
mean-tempered drunk. Bree tells me that he's rough with
women. That could be what happened to Aspen."

Miguel had considered that possibility. Aspen's disappearance might not be part of the ongoing Del Gardo investigation. Emma's cousin was beautiful; she might have
been the victim of a simple assault by a local *cabron.* "Why
would he go after a woman with a baby in the backseat?
Why run her off the road?"

"Good questions," the sheriff said. "And why would
Emma link Aspen's disappearance with Del Gardo?"

Miguel grinned at the phone. "I'd almost forgotten that you consider Emma's visions to be valid evidence."

"Admit it, smart guy. So do you."

Miguel looked into the kitchen, where Emma had finished off her first glass of wine and reached for the bottle to pour another. A bit of color had returned to her cheeks.

"I believe in her," he said. "Emma doesn't lie, but some of these visions are *muy loco*."

"See you soon." Martinez disconnected the call.

Miguel returned to the table and sat beside her. The wine seemed to be already having an effect on Emma. The worry lines between her eyes were gone, and she wore a crooked smile.

"I was thinking," she said. "What if the fiesta doesn't have anything to do with the investigation? What if it's meant as a personal message to me?"

"And what would that message be?"

"A cautionary tale." She took another deep sip of wine. "Even when I think I'm having fun, like at a party, it's dangerous. The singing can turn dark. The dancing gets frantic and terrible. Maybe I'm simply not meant to be twirling around in a purple dress."

"What are you meant for?"

"Talking to dead people and writing novels of pulse-pounding adventure." She set her wineglass on the table and shook her head. "I don't mean to sound like I'm feeling sorry for myself. I have a good life. I've been doing this for years, and I'm perfectly content living by myself."

He took her hand. "But you don't live alone. You have little *mijo*."

"Jack is only here until we find Aspen. When she comes back, her baby will go home with her."

"You're not alone," he said. "You have me."

He would never allow Emma—a beautiful flower—to

wither alone and untended. His job was to show her the sun and watch as she bloomed. He stood and gently pulled her to her feet.

"What are you doing?" she asked.

"Teaching you to dance." Though she balked, he held both of her hands firmly. "Simple salsa. Three steps."

"This is silly," she said. "I've always been a klutz, and I don't need to know how to—"

"Everyone needs to dance. It's part of being human. If you want, I can quote anthropological evidence to prove it."

"And it's all about the data. Right?"

"Step forward on your right foot," he said. "At the same time, pick up the left. That's the first step."

Reluctantly, she did as he asked. "Now what?"

"Put your left foot down and put your weight on it. That's the second step."

"Okay," she said.

"Now bring your right foot back so it's even with the left. That's three."

Her feet, in purple socks, moved as he instructed. When she had the simple move down, he matched his steps to hers and counted the beat. "One, two, three. And one, two, three."

He showed her variations on the basic step. Going backward instead of forward. Twice forward. Twice back. "You've got it, Emma. You can dance."

"I can step," she corrected him. "But this doesn't look anything like the salsa dancing I've seen."

"So we add the hip action." He showed her the simple step, moving his hips in time to nonexistent music. Dancing and music came easily to him. "Feel the beat going through your body." He added a shoulder motion and clapped his hands. "One, two, three. And, one, two, three."

She attempted the move, clumsy at first. After a few

tries, her body understood the simple rhythm. Holding hands, they moved together.

"You're dancing," he said, still keeping the beat. "And nothing terrible is happening."

"One, two, three, and…" she counted under her breath.

He twirled her. "Hot move, *chica*. You're not meant to be alone."

"Don't confuse me."

"Relax. Feel the beat."

He pulled her against him. Their bodies moved as one, hips undulating. The tips of her breasts grazed his chest. He tossed his head, and she did the same. Her straight, brown hair flipped across her face.

He cinched her body tightly against his. Purposely, he slowed the count. *"Uno, dos, tres…"*

Her blue eyes flashed. Her lips parted.

Before he could kiss her, the doorbell sounded.

They split apart.

"That must be the sheriff," she said.

Miguel strode through the house, deactivated the alarm and unfastened the dead bolt.

Sheriff Martinez glared through the screen door. "This time, your brother has gone too far."

## Chapter Sixteen

Miguel never claimed to be his twin brother's keeper. Dylan was a force unto himself. According to Sheriff Martinez, Dylan and his FBI buddy, Ben Parrish, had entered reservation territory, had gone to the home of Sherman Watts and had busted their way inside. An FBI raid. Totally unauthorized.

"Here's what they found," Martinez said angrily. "Nothing. Watts wasn't there."

The physical presence of their suspect was only part of the story. Miguel seriously doubted that Watts's home was void of evidence. "Did they have a chance to look around?"

"Bree and the tribal cops caught up with them pretty fast. She told them to get the hell off Ute property. The FBI has no jurisdiction on the rez. Your brother's lucky she didn't charge him with breaking and entering."

"Is Bree in charge?"

"Oh, yeah." Martinez had the look of a man who was about to get his butt kicked by his fiancée.

"I want to talk to her," Miguel said.

He needed to convince Bree to let him make a thorough analysis of the scene. Even if there wasn't anything as obvious as a smoking gun, there could be prints, fabrics, notes—some detail that would give them a lead.

Martinez took off his hat and raked his fingers through his hair. "Bree has good cause to be angry. Law enforcement in the Four Corners area is hard enough with four states vying for jurisdiction. Much less the FBI."

"Dylan messed up," Miguel agreed.

The deputy who had accompanied Martinez placed the food from the Morning Ray Café on the kitchen table and handed Miguel his guitar.

*"Gracias,"* Miguel said to the deputy. He turned to the sheriff. "I need to get inside Watts's house. Bridger said Watts had a partner. We need to figure out who that is. If I could explain to Bree—"

"Miguel, you don't know how mad that woman is. She'll chew your face off."

"I could talk to her," Emma offered.

When Miguel looked into her cornflower-blue eyes, it was hard to remember that Emma was part Ute. The way she'd handled Jerry Burch showed that she knew her way around the rez. But gaining access to the scene was Miguel's problem. "This is my job. I've worked with Bree before. We can be reasonable with each other. One law enforcement professional to another."

"It's your funeral," Martinez said.

Still, he got Bree on his cell phone and handed it to Miguel. Her first words weren't encouraging. "I can't believe I'm talking to anyone named Acevedo."

"My brother made a mistake," Miguel readily admitted. "He's not a patient man. Believe me, I know. I grew up with that *vato*."

"Here's the deal, Miguel. I don't give a damn about protecting the rights of scum like Sherman Watts. And you know I'm willing to cooperate with the crime lab."

"I know," he said.

"But this is out of my hands. The tribal council doesn't

want the FBI thinking they can storm onto our land without consent."

"We'll be fast and respectful," he said. "Let me clean up my brother's mess. Close off the house. My forensic team can be on the road in five minutes."

"I've already secured the house," she said. "It's closed off and I have a man posted outside. But I need a clear directive from the council before you or anybody else gets near this place."

"Watts is connected to our ongoing investigation. And in the murder of Vincent Del Gardo," he said. "We have evidence that could match up to items in his house."

"How did Watts become a suspect?"

He told her about the trip he and Emma took to the rez, explained about the leather necklace and their interview with Jerry Burch. Then, he added the clincher. "More than anything, this is about finding Aspen Meadows, a missing daughter of your tribe."

After a pause, Bree said, "Next time, you set one toe into my jurisdiction, let me know. In the meantime, I'll see what I can do to convince the tribal council to give access to your forensic team. Probably not until tomorrow." She paused again. "From what I hear, you and Emma are getting close."

He shot a gaze toward the woman he'd held in his arms only a moment ago. "That's true."

"If you hurt her, Miguel, I'll track you down like a dog and kick your butt."

"Good to know."

He handed the phone back to Martinez and went toward Emma. Though she considered herself to be a loner, she had a lot of friends. "Bree says hi."

"Is she going to let you investigate?"

"It's up to the tribal council."

Emma groaned. "It could take hours for them to make a decision."

Time they didn't have. The threats to Emma's safety seemed to grow with every minute that passed. Bridger had reason to want her dead. Watts was involved in her cousin's disappearance and might come after Emma if he thought she was close to finding Aspen. Not to mention the un-named partner of Sherman Watts.

They were like sharks, circling her tidy little house in Kenner City, and he was only one man with a gun. He couldn't stop a coordinated attack from Watts and his partner. Nor could he deal with an explosive device lobbed through a window. Half a dozen other disaster scenarios flashed through his mind.

One thing was clear: to deal with these sharks, they were going to need a bigger boat.

As soon as the sheriff got off the phone, Miguel explained the worsening situation. "I need two of your men. One at the front door. Another at the back."

"Okay, for tonight. But I can't promise bodyguards twenty-four hours a day. I don't have the manpower."

Tomorrow, Miguel might be able to pull in other guards using people from the lab. But bodyguard duty wasn't their training. They were technicians, scientists. What he needed was a man of action, someone who was dying to kick ass, a marksman who was trained in protection.

He needed his brother, Dylan.

AFTER THEY HAD DINNER and finished off the bottle of wine, Emma checked on Jack who, remarkably, hadn't wakened in spite of all the commotion made by Sheriff Martinez. The baby slept so soundly that she rested her hand on his back to make sure he was still breathing. When he wiggled, she quickly pulled her hand away.

It was too early for him to be down for the night, and she worried that Jack would be wide-awake at two in the morning, disrupting her sleep and Miguel's. Still, she couldn't bring herself to wake him. Leaning over the crib, she kissed Jack above his perfectly shaped ear and whispered, "Your mama will be home soon. We're going to find her."

Was that a promise she could keep? Her latest vision had resulted in useful information. She'd given Sheriff Martinez the names of Bridger's two prior victims— Simone Caparelli and Burton Nestor. And she was certain that Bridger had killed Del Gardo. But she couldn't figure out how those crimes linked up with Aspen's disappearance. Unless she was missing a clue from her vision... The mariachi music? The sombreros?

Sherman Watts was the more likely lead. She sensed the aura of danger around him, sensed that he was the man who had been chasing Aspen near the river. Also, there was the fact that Watts's bear claw necklace was found near Aspen's car.

The light strumming from Miguel's guitar led her into the front room. He sat on the edge of the rocking chair tuning his six-stringed instrument. The golden wood of the body gleamed softly in the light from a table lamp with a beaded shade.

Without disturbing him, she lowered herself onto the sofa and stretched out her legs. In her mind, she took a snapshot of this moment, hoping always to remember Miguel as he concentrated on his guitar. His hair fell loose across his forehead. He'd taken off his outer denim shirt. His black T-shirt revealed strong forearms and wrists that tapered to his long, sensitive fingers. Like her, he'd taken off his shoes and was barefoot.

When he looked up at her, she noticed the silver medallion that hung at his throat. Without looking down, he plucked the strings in a classical melody.

Emma wasn't a musical person, but she knew what she liked. And she definitely enjoyed the subtle blending of sound that came from his guitar. The vibration of the strings resonated inside her.

When he paused, she said one word. "Beautiful."

"Better than the Mozart you play for *mijo?*"

"Much better."

"Actually, that was Mozart. An adaptation of a piano adagio."

Could he possible be more perfect? "How did you start playing the guitar?"

"I was about twelve. My uncle got a new guitar and gave me his old one." He continued to finger the strings. "At first, I thought I should be in a band. Figured it was a good way to get girls. Every *chica* loves a rock star. But my uncle told me that this was an expensive guitar and I shouldn't play around with it."

He tapped a rapid tattoo on the body of the instrument as he continued. "Don't play around? That's what I said to him. What else are you supposed to do with a guitar?"

"And then?" she asked.

"He showed me. My uncle is a good musician. He taught me a lot. Then I took some other classes."

"The lessons paid off." She exhaled a contented sigh. Though there were deputies posted at the front of the house and the back, she felt like they were in a special, secluded space. A private world.

Miguel grinned. "My guitar still didn't help me get a date."

While he held the guitar, she could feel him opening up to her. "Ever since we met, I've been wanting to ask you about something."

"Go ahead."

"That medallion you always wear, it's from Santuario de Chimayo in New Mexico," she said. "I've never been there, but I've heard of it."

"It's a place of miracles," he said, accompanying his words on the guitar. "Long ago, a friar from Chimayo discovered a mysterious crucifix buried in the earth. He took it with him to Santa Cruz, but the crucifix disappeared. He found it back in the original hole where it was buried. This happened twice. A small adobe church was built on the site where the crucifix was found. Later, it was discovered that those who came to worship were cured of their ills."

"By praying to the crucifix?"

"By the dirt," he said. "The sacred soil from El Posito—the pit where the crucifix was found—has healing powers."

She raised a skeptical eyebrow. "I'm surprised that a guy like you, a scientist, believes in miracles."

"Hey, I was an altar boy." He stopped playing and held the medallion between thumb and forefinger. "Some things can't be explained by facts. Like your gift."

"Talking to the dead? I'm not so sure it's a gift."

"Your visions can't be rationally dissected. I can't put them under a microscope or through a computer program, but I believe you see them."

When she first saw him standing on her doorstep, watching her through suspicious eyes, Emma never would have predicted that he would accept her so completely.

Throughout her life, she'd been made to feel like she was weird or different. "You don't think I'm a witch? A *bruja?* Or mentally disturbed?"

"For sure, you're crazy," he teased. "*Loca bonita.* But crazy in a good way."

"Do I have Chimayo to thank for your open-mindedness?"

"Chimayo changed me," he admitted. "When I was growing up, I was nearly as wild as Dylan. *Dos perros,* we were like two dogs out howling at the moon. I got in a fight, got shot."

"My God, how old were you?"

"Sixteen." He shrugged. "Just a flesh wound in my shoulder, but we were a long way from the doctor. I lost a lot of blood. For a few minutes, I was dead. Then I went into a coma."

"You saw the light," she said.

"Pure white. Like angel's wings." His eyes took on a dreamy expression. "I was at peace. I wanted to stay in that beautiful place, but my mama wasn't ready for me to die. She went to Chimayo and brought back the soil from El Posito, which she rubbed into my hand."

"And you woke up?"

"A day later." He strummed his guitar for emphasis. "The doctor said I would have come out of the coma, with or without the soil. But it was important to me. And to Mama. She'd already lost one child."

"Your sister," she said. "Teresa."

His gaze rested gently on her face. "You've seen her."

"Dressed in white," Emma said, remembering her vision of the lovely young woman. "She wants you to know that she's all right."

"I miss her. Will always miss her. She was killed a few months after her *quinceanera*. An accidental shooting. After her death, Dylan and I went even crazier than before. It's probably why I got myself shot."

She knew that grief took many forms. Sometimes, people came to her, looking for their loved ones who had passed away. Often, they were angry. They wanted to curse the dead person for leaving them alone. "You were angry."

"Angry at death. I was only sixteen but living on the edge, taunting death. If fate could take my sister—a good girl who never did harm to anyone—I dared death to take me, too."

"And got yourself shot," she said.

"*Muy stupido.* I think Teresa's murder is what made Dylan decide to go into the FBI."

"And you?" she asked. "What did you decide?"

"I was different after my coma. More serious. I got into medical science and thought I might become a doctor. That's when I went to Chimayo myself and got this medallion. On the back, it says, Protect and Heal."

"But you went into forensics instead."

He played a chord on his guitar. "And that's the story of Miguel Acevedo. A rational man who believes in miracles."

The perfect man for her. At this moment, she felt so close to him. She knew that she was meant to be with him. Her virginity and lack of experience in lovemaking weren't an issue. She knew Miguel would understand. He'd be gentle.

"Now," he said, "we get back to work. I have this guitar for a reason. In your vision you heard mariachi music. If we can figure out what they were playing, the lyrics might be a clue."

But she wasn't interested in deciphering clues. She wanted to make love. "I already told you. The Mexican Hat Dance."

"Here's another." His fingers plucked out a familiar song.

"La Cucaracha," she said. "Yes, they played that. But I can't think of any clue that might relate to a cockroach."

"Unless it refers to Sherman Watts," he said.

He changed the rhythm. His left hand darted along the frets while he picked out individual notes on the strings. In a warm tenor, he sang in Spanish, the ballad of "Malagueña."

She leaned back against the sofa and closed her eyes. His voice mesmerized her. Though she didn't understand the lyrics, a plaintive tone of desperation and yearning touched her heart. Unexpected tears burned behind her eyelids.

He finished with a dramatic guitar flourish. "Well, Emma? Was this song in your vision?"

She pushed herself off the sofa and stood. "Tell me the words."

"A lover sings the praises of his Malagueña. He longs for her. Without her love, he will surely die of grief."

She stood before him. "We can't let that happen. Lovers are meant to be together."

He set his guitar aside and pulled her tight against him.

# Chapter Seventeen

Still hearing the echo of his music inside her head, Emma submitted to her desires. She kissed Miguel with a passion so intense that it seemed to lift her off her feet. He cinched his arm around her waist as if to anchor her. He deepened the kiss with his tongue. Sensation raced through her veins.

She wanted to savor every touch, to fully experience this moment. But it was all happening so fast. They fell into an embrace on the sofa. He rose above her, his eyes shimmering like emerald stars, and she was overwhelmed. Unable to think, she didn't know what to do or what move to make next.

Doubt crept in. Was her inexperience showing? Would she make a fool of herself?

As if sensing her hesitation, Miguel spoke. "I've wanted this since the first time I saw you."

"Me, too."

He stroked her cheek, and she did the same to him. When his hand glided down her throat to her breast, an amazing thing happened. Her body reacted to his caresses as if she knew exactly what she was doing. She responded on pure instinct.

When he took off her shirt and her bra, she felt no shame. Not even when his gaze lingered on her breasts. He touched her as gently and skillfully as he stroked the strings of his guitar.

Again, she responded. Though she'd never done this dance before, she trusted him to take the lead. The rest of their clothing slipped away, almost like a miracle.

She placed her hand on his bronzed chest. His lean muscles quivered.

"Truly," he whispered as he kissed her again. "You are a crazy and beautiful lady."

"I must be crazy."

"And beautiful," he said. "Don't forget beautiful."

She didn't protest this extravagant compliment because she knew his sincerity was real. Miguel wouldn't lie. He thought she was beautiful, and she felt like the most fantastic creature on the planet.

Their bodies glided together. The rhythm of passion grew inside her—a throbbing, inexorable beat that would not be denied. He stroked between her legs, creating a new tempo, a trembling counterpoint.

When he paused to sheath himself in a condom he took from his wallet, she could hardly stand the brief moment away from him. She'd been waiting for this moment for a very long time. All her life.

He poised above her, gazing down. Slowly, slowly, he entered her. Her breath caught. She was on the verge of fainting but, at the same time, intensely involved with each thrust. This was more than she'd imagined. Better.

His body tensed. At that very second, she was rocked by surging emotions, like being caught in a churning ocean wave and tumbled to the shore.

They climaxed together—a thrill and a relief. She must have done something right.

Breathing hard, they lay tangled together on the narrow sofa. Fireworks burst behind her closed eyelids. She reveled in the sensations, taking a full measure of enjoyment. And then, she sighed. "That was worth waiting for."

"Worthwhile," he said.

"If I'd known…" Her voice trailed off. "I'm a virgin, Miguel."

"What?"

She opened her eyes. "I mean, I *was* a virgin. Used to be. Until just a few minutes ago. You're my first lover." Amused, she rolled the word in her mouth. "Looov-ah."

His gaze darted, but he didn't move away from her. "I didn't know."

Of course, he didn't know. Virginity was her secret. Perhaps she shouldn't have mentioned anything, but he'd been open with her. It didn't seem right to hold back. "You couldn't tell, could you? Did I make mistakes?"

"No mistakes, *querida*." He kissed her forehead. "You were perfect."

She cleared her throat. "I'd like to do it again."

"That can be arranged."

However, before they had progressed beyond one kiss, she heard Jack fussing in the bedroom. As she'd feared, the baby wasn't going to sleep well tonight.

She eased away from the wonderfully cozy spot on the sofa beside him and went to care for the baby, gathering her clothing along the way. After slipping into a nightshirt, Emma performed the familiar baby care routine—changing his diaper, wiping and powdering. These were actions she'd done hundreds of times. And yet, as she lifted the baby to her shoulder, she was aware of the difference. Her life had changed. More than the slight tingling between her legs, she felt an afterglow of the passion she'd shared with Miguel. Not a virgin anymore.

She wished she could call Aspen and tell her.

LYING ON THE SOFA, Miguel took a moment to digest Emma's secret. A virgin? How could a woman as beautiful as Emma be a thirty-year-old virgin? She'd talked about being an outcast on the rez, about going off to college when she was only sixteen, about working alone in her office. But a virgin?

As the first man who had slept with her, he felt a certain responsibility. This couldn't be a one-night stand. He couldn't hop onto his motorcycle and ride off into the sunset.

Not that he had considered either of those alternatives. From the start, he knew that he wanted something more with Emma. A relationship with her would be a constant amazement.

He pulled himself off the sofa. This was all working out for the best.

While she fed *mijo,* he stayed with her, playing his guitar and thinking of the next time they would make love. He'd be more careful with her. He'd tenderly introduce her to the pleasures of her own body.

After his feeding, Jack was wide-awake. His schedule had been disrupted, and he wasn't about to let them rest when he wanted to play. It took over an hour to get him back to sleep.

Miguel collapsed on the bed beside her. He could tell that she was exhausted. Gently, he kissed her smooth forehead. "Tonight, we'll sleep. Tomorrow, we'll make love again."

Her blue eyes, lined with black lashes, gleamed in the faint light of the bedside lamp. She whispered his name. "Tomorrow is a very long time to wait."

"Hours." Having her so close, lying beside her on the bed, he was already aroused. But he wouldn't push her.

She coiled her arms around him and pulled him closer. "I can't wait until tomorrow, Miguel. I want you."

She'd gone from virgin to wild cat. He couldn't have been happier.

After they made love, he closed his eyes and sank into dreams of Emma that lasted until early morning when Jack was awake again.

MIGUEL EXPECTED THIS to be a very long day. With luck, he would be given permission from Bree to process the scene at the home of Sherman Watts. New evidence could be uncovered.

With Jack tucked into the crook of his arm, he made his first phone call to his brother. "Dylan, I need you at Emma's house."

"Why? What's your problem, *vato?*"

His tone was surly, and Miguel answered in kind. "After what you did last night, you should take a step back from this investigation. I need a bodyguard for Emma and little *mijo.*"

"I'm not a babysitter."

"Maybe you should be. That's something you can do right."

Miguel imagined his twin seething. Dylan wasn't accustomed to failure. Tersely, he said, "I'll be there."

He watched Emma as she bustled around her kitchen, putting together trays of coffee and cereal for the two deputies who had spent the night guarding her house. She wore a cotton shirt the color of lilacs in spring, and she reminded him of a graceful flower, bobbing in the mountain breezes. Such poetry! She inspired him. *Te quiero,* Emma. He thought the words but didn't say them.

Once, he noticed her laughing to herself. Was she talking to her ghosts? Telling them that she was no longer a virgin?

Unexpectedly, she bounced over to him and kissed his cheek. "Don't look so worried, Miguel. Everything is going to be all right. We'll find Aspen. Soon. I can feel it."

"You've been talking to your ghosts again."

She shrugged. "I just have a feeling."

A bizarre and disturbing thought occurred to him. "Last night, when we were making love—"

"Twice," she reminded him with a sexy grin.

"*Sí*, both times when we were making love, were we…alone?"

She cocked her head to one side and gave him a quizzical look. "Of course, we were."

"I mean *completely* alone." He gestured to the air around them. "No ghosts."

She gave a throaty laugh. "Did you think my grandma and Aunt Rose might be around?"

The thought of two little old lady spectators made him cringe. "They have a habit of popping in unannounced."

"Not to worry. They come to me in response to something I'm thinking about." She glided her arms up his chest and around his neck. "Last night, my every thought focused on you."

He gave her a quick peck on the cheek. "You're sure?"

"Positive."

His cell phone rang, and he disentangled himself to answer. It was Callie at the crime lab. After she gave him an update on their progress, she had another proposition. "I'd like to have you bring Emma over here."

He figured that Callie wanted to see baby Jack again, but that wasn't going to happen. After last night's fussing, it was obvious that they needed to keep *mijo* on a more regular schedule. "The baby needs his rest."

"This isn't about Jack," she said. "Emma is a valuable resource that we haven't been using. I want her to take a look at the evidence. Maybe she'll get a sense of where to go from here."

"We'll be over later," he said. "Any word from Bree

on whether or not we can go onto the rez to process Watts's house?"

"Nothing yet."

After ending his call, he paced through the house, carrying Jack and thinking. He expected that the evidence they'd find at Watts's house would point to a partnership with Boyd Perkins. In prior investigation, the crime lab had already found fingerprints and a bullet from a gun owned by Perkins. Their operating assumption was that Perkins— a known hit man for another Vegas crime ring—had been sent to this area to kill Del Gardo. It seemed rational to assume that Perkins had hooked up with Watts—a man who knew the territory.

After he put Jack down for a nap, Miguel tried to discuss this possibility with Emma. But she wasn't interested in talk. In spite of the deputies in the kitchen, she shoved the bedroom door closed. The intensity of her kiss shocked and amazed him.

It seemed that her intention was to make up for thirty years of virginity in one day. Which was okay by him. The next time he left the house, he'd pick up a crate of condoms.

IT WAS AFTER LUNCH when Miguel opened the door for his brother. As soon as their eyes met, Miguel knew Dylan was *muy furioso*. That attitude always meant trouble.

Carrying his cardboard cup of coffee, Dylan strode through the house. Wearing his FBI jacket with the letters stenciled on the back, he wasn't exactly undercover. "I've been ordered to stand down. For the rest of the day, I'm supposed to back off."

"What did you expect?"

"I expected to catch Watts." He pivoted on his heel and glared. "It's what you should have done."

Miguel knew better than to get into a spitting match with

his twin, but he couldn't let that statement stand. "You think I should have gone after Watts?"

"As soon as you had the suspect's name, you should have taken action."

Not when Emma and Jack were in the car with him. Should he have dragged an infant into a dangerous situation? "I did take action. Big mistake. I called you."

Dylan set down his coffee on the dining-room table where Jack sat in his baby seat, waving his arms and kicking his legs like a swimmer who didn't know he was out of the water.

Turning away from the baby, Dylan faced him. He tore off his jacket and squared his shoulders, ready for a fight. "If I had been where you were—on the rez—I would have made my move. Watts would be in custody."

"Listen to me, *estupido*. If I had—"

"Don't call me stupid."

"What else would you call your unauthorized raid?"

"At least, I did something," Dylan said.

"Something stupid."

*Are we in grade school?* His twin had always known how to provoke him. Miguel's fingers curled into fists. It'd be dumb to get into a fight in Emma's dining room, but punching Dylan would feel so damned good.

"Here's how I see it," Dylan lectured. "The only way to nab Watts—a *gallito* who knows every hiding place in these hills and valleys—is to strike fast. Grab him before he figures out we're onto him."

"Grab him? Even when you have no authority on the rez to make an arrest."

"Jurisdiction be damned," Dylan said. "You know this guy was involved in Aspen's disappearance, right?"

"That's right," Emma said as she entered from the kitchen. Fearlessly, she positioned herself between them. "Watts is the man I saw in my vision. We found his necklace near the place where Aspen lost control of her car. He's definitely involved."

"He's the best lead we have. *Dios mio,* he's the only lead."

"Is that so?" Emma shot him a hostile glare that told Miguel she'd been eavesdropping. "My, Dylan. It almost sounds like you're actually beginning to care about what happened to my cousin."

"Yes, I care." His voice was strained. "I care about Aspen. And Julie. And even Del Gardo. I want this case closed."

"We all do," Miguel said. "But you've been warned off. You need to take a step back."

"Are you telling me what to do?"

"Leave this to me, Dylan."

"You? You've never even made an arrest." Dylan stuck out his chin, a tempting target. "Oh, maybe you've read a suspect his Miranda rights after he's been taken into custody. But you don't know what it's like in the field."

"Kicking down doors. Racing in hot pursuit. Waving your gun." Miguel's anger simmered, close to boiling over. "That's not my job."

"Because you hide in the lab. You stay safe."

"I stay smart. I think before I act."

There were times—plenty of times—when he'd prefer the release of action. If anyone threatened Emma or baby Jack, he'd be hard-pressed to hold himself in check.

He glanced over at her, where she stood watching their argument like a spectator at a tennis match. Then, he turned back to his brother. "Kicking ass? That's the easy part."

"You think my job is easy?"

"Not when it's done right," Miguel fired back. "It's tough to put together enough evidence for a conviction. You know that, Dylan. You know that when you angered the tribal elders, you made everybody's job harder. Because of you, we can't get into Watts's house and do the forensics."

"I was just trying to—"

"You didn't even apprehend the suspect."

Dylan winced. The fight went out of him as he dropped into a chair beside the table. His gaze cast downward. He was in pain—genuine pain. And Miguel felt his agony.

A few seconds ago, he'd wanted to punch his brother in the nose. Instead, he rested a comforting hand on Dylan's shoulder. "It'll work out. We'll get this guy."

Looking up, Dylan's face was troubled. "I lied just now when I said I don't make mistakes. Some of the stuff I've done is beyond fixing. I'll never make it right."

Miguel assumed he was referring to a serial killer case he'd been on before coming to Kenner City. Though his brother hadn't told him details, he knew that case had been intense. "Whatever you need, I'm here."

He stood and gave him a hug. No matter how much they fought, they were part of each other. Twins.

Over his brother's shoulder, he saw Emma smiling warmly. She'd fit well into the Acevedo family, where passions ran high but they never stopped caring for each other.

Dylan stepped back. "Okay, Miguel. What do you want me to do?"

He pointed to Jack. "This little *mijo* has been through hell. He's lost his mama. He's been dragged all over the countryside looking for bad guys. Today, he needs rest and the best protection the FBI can provide."

"You weren't joking? You really want me to spend the day as a babysitter?"

"That's right."

Dylan lifted Jack from his baby seat. When Jack burst into a spontaneous grin, Dylan had to respond. "I care about this case," he murmured. "More than you know."

## *Chapter Eighteen*

At the crime lab, Emma stood beside Miguel and watched while Ava and Bobby displayed the bagged and tagged evidence they'd gathered from inside Del Gardo's tunnels. Supposedly, Callie wanted Emma here as a resource—a psychic translator of these physical clues. She hoped she could help, but the debris from the tunnels looked like garbage to her.

Ava held up plastic evidence bags containing candy wrappers, an empty aspirin bottle, used tissues and a personal music player. "Because of fingerprints, we assume all these items belonged to Del Gardo. Emma, is there anything here you'd like to look at more closely?"

Bobby O'Shea watched her with a curiosity that was both insulting and flattering. He asked, "Exactly what do you need to get your vision started? Should we hand you things in a certain order?"

"She's not a psychic computer," Miguel informed his colleagues. "Emma gets her insights from people who have passed away. Sometimes they cooperate. Sometimes, not. These ghosts are as unpredictable as the weather."

She smiled at him—Miguel, her lover. Her first lover. Being with him made it difficult to concentrate on anything else, but she had to try. For Aspen's sake. "I wish I could guarantee accuracy, but it doesn't work that way. It might be best if I just watch while you show Miguel the evidence."

"Okay," Miguel said as he looked over the array. "From this stuff, we can deduce that Del Gardo liked chocolate with peanuts and probably had a head cold. What did you get from the music player?"

"Frank Sinatra, Tony Bennett and jazz," Ava said.

"Tell me about the prints."

"Almost all were from Del Gardo. Likewise with DNA extracted from hairs we found on the bedroll."

"But his head was shaved," Emma said.

Ava stroked her own chin. "From his white beard."

Callie joined them. "The Santa Claus beard. It's hard to believe that such a simple disguise was so effective. When I saw his body in autopsy, I barely recognized him." She gave Emma a quick nod. "Thank you for coming."

"I hope I can help."

"I have a bit of good news," Callie said. "I just got off the phone with Sheriff Martinez. He said that the Colorado state patrol sighted Bridger's black SUV outside Telluride."

"Yes!" Emma gave a fist pump, a gesture she'd never before used in her life. "He's on the run."

"Was he arrested?" Miguel asked.

"Afraid not."

Callie's expression was troubled, and Emma sensed an undercurrent of strong emotion. Patting Callie's shoulder, she said, "You must be relieved. Del Gardo is no longer a threat to your safety."

"I've been worrying about him for months, looking over my shoulder, never knowing when he might attack. And yet, there's something poignant about the death of an adversary." She picked an invisible piece of lint off her white lab coat. "It's hard to believe he's finally gone."

Miguel nudged Bobby's shoulder. "What else did you find in the tunnels?"

"Not the millions of dollars in treasure. Ain't that a shame." A goofy grin made his face look lopsided. "I already figured out how I'd spend my share."

"You don't get a share," Callie said. "We're not treasure hunters."

"Beagles," Bobby said. "I read about this guy online who made a fortune raising and training purebred German shepherds. I could do the same thing. Buy a couple of acres and set up a beagle ranch."

"Bobby," Miguel interrupted. "The evidence."

"Right. There are other prints, mostly smudged and probably old. From clerks in stores. Stuff like that." He shuffled through evidence bags until he found one containing a plastic comb. "This is the prize. A nice, clear thumbprint from our Vegas hit man—Boyd Perkins."

"Unfortunately," Ava said, "one print isn't enough to draw conclusions. We can't say for sure that Perkins was in the tunnels. Del Gardo might have picked up the comb."

"That print shows Perkins was close," Bobby said. "That's significant."

"But did Perkins kill the old fox?" Miguel posed the question. "What else does the evidence say?"

On this topic, Emma needed no further validation from the physical evidence. Because of her vision, she was certain that Bridger was the man who murdered Del Gardo. She'd seen Bridger with blood on his hands. As the memory flashed in her mind, she heard echoes of the fiesta music.

The raucous sounds of the mariachis faded into the sweet resonance of Miguel's guitar playing, the memory of his voice singing softly. She thought of his skillful hands, plucking the strings of his guitar and caressing her body. A rush of passion coursed through her veins, raising her temperature. She fanned her face.

"Are you all right?" Callie asked.

"I'm great," she said. And she meant it. Emma was no longer a timid old maid. Not a loner anymore.

"Over here," Ava said as she led the way across the lab to the evidence wall where several items were displayed. "I've made a preliminary sketch of the inside of the tunnels. As you can see, it's very similar to the VDG map made by Julie Grainger."

Emma compared the two drawings. It was obvious that Julie had been in those tunnels. Had Del Gardo found her snooping around in his lair? Had he killed her?

Though Julie's murder was important to Emma, her focus remained on her cousin. She needed to know how Aspen fit into the picture that was emerging from the evidence. Moving along the wall, she studied the other information that had been posted. A map of Kenner County and the reservation took up a large portion of the wall. Various locations had been labeled. Griffin's house. The spot where Aspen's car was found. Sherman Watts's house. He seemed to be equal distance from Towaoc, the casino on the reservation and a little town just outside the rez called Mexican Hat.

Her gaze moved down the board to a series of mug shots, labeled with tags—a Rogue's Gallery of suspects. She saw Bridger with his several aliases listed. And two photos of Del Gardo: a death shot of an old man with a beard and a picture of what he looked like without his disguise. Comparing the two, she decided that Vincent Del Gardo was definitely more sinister with hair.

Emma barely glanced at Boyd Perkins. Though central to the investigation, he didn't make much of an impression on her. Sherman Watts was different. His flat, black eyes seemed to follow her as she moved. He looked older than she thought, probably in his late forties. Hard living had carved deep lines in his face. Danger emanated from him.

Farther down the wall were photos of Simone Capparelli and Burton Nestor, easily recognizable as her two ghosts—the victims of Bridger. She pointed to them. "Did you find any information about these two?"

"We checked with Las Vegas homicide," Callie said. "Both of these murders are open investigations. Bridger was interrogated, but he had airtight alibis for both incidents."

Now would have been a good time for Simone and Burton to appear. Emma gazed intently at the photos. All she had was a memory of her vision where these two victims danced at the fiesta.

"There's something I want to see," Miguel said. "The cast of the boot print we found near Del Gardo's body."

"Got it." Bobby's grin couldn't get any wider. Clearly, he was proud of his work. As he loped toward a computer, Emma was reminded of one of the beagles Bobby hoped to raise.

He tapped on the keyboard. "Here are the digital photos we took at the scene. Check out the surrounding area. It's all bushes, shrubs and rocks. We were lucky to get this boot print."

Bobby scrolled through a photo array. Pictures taken from every angle. Several included measuring instruments placed beside the print to indicate the size in inches and centimeters.

"It's a size thirteen," Bobby said. "Big foot."

Miguel leaned closer to the screen. "The heel box doesn't look like any cowboy boot I've ever seen."

"That's right," Bobby said. "These boots weren't made for riding. They're meant to be stylish. Custom-crafted."

He rose from his seat at the computer. With a flourish,

he unveiled the cast he'd made of the footprint. Emma reached over to touch the surface. "It's perfect. How did you get so much detail?"

"It's a diestone material. Mix the powder up, pour it in, let it set. And then spray with sealant."

"This would be great for arts and crafts projects," she said. "I could make little prints of Jack's hands and feet."

Callie beamed. "How is my favorite baby?"

"Taking a day off to rest. Dylan is watching him."

"He ought to be good at babysitting," Callie muttered. "He acts like he's about two years old."

Emma suppressed a chuckle. "I have the feeling that Dylan was one of those kids who never learned to play well with others."

"Hey," Miguel interrupted. "Can we focus on the case?"

"I saved the best for last," Bobby said. "Remember how I said the boots were custom? They're also new, barely worn. I checked with the Las Vegas PD, and they referred me to Ostrich Al's Custom Shoes. When I described the boot print to Al, he didn't even need to check his records. Two weeks ago, he sold a pair of snakeskin boots, size thirteen, to Hank Bridger."

That was enough proof for Emma. "So we know he was there. At the tunnels. We know he killed Del Gardo."

"Not necessarily," Miguel said. "We've placed him at the crime scene, but we still need to put the gun in his hand."

"I wonder if he knew," she mused, "how close he was."

"To what?" Callie asked.

"Bridger is obsessed with Julie's map, thinks it will show him where the money is hidden. If he knew that map was of the tunnels, he'd be there right now. With a shovel and a pickax."

She turned to see Miguel watching her. "Bridger wouldn't go back there now. We have the area marked off as a crime scene."

"But we're done with forensics," Bobby said. "And we don't have a guard posted."

"Bridger and the tunnels," Emma said. "They go together like…"

Tongue-tied, she tried to come up with an apt comparison. She was, after all, a writer of pulse-pounding adventure, and she ought to have a ready phrase. But when she looked into Miguel's green eyes, the only simile she could come up with was her and Miguel. They belonged together. Their names should be carved in the trunk of a tree with a big, sappy heart drawn around them.

She felt a blush creeping up her throat, and she shrugged. "That's my hunch."

"Bridger and the tunnels," Miguel said. "I'll remember that."

He turned to the others, and they discussed other evidence that was yet to be processed. Though Miguel had been absent for most of the work at the crime lab, he was clearly in charge of analyzing the crime scene evidence. Was there anything sexier than a competent man? Anyone sexier than Miguel?

Listening to their discussion with only half an ear, she turned back to the wall. She touched the VDG map, hoping she'd make a connection with Julie. The spirit of the deceased FBI agent had led her into the investigation. It made sense that Julie would show the next step.

Everyone else was working hard, putting forth an intense effort. Emma had nothing but the echo of that annoying mariachi tune. She must have been humming it because Callie came closer. "What's that song?"

"Something I've got stuck in my head," Emma said. "I heard the tune in a vision, and it keeps playing over and over."

"Could be significant," Callie said.

"I don't think so. It's a kid's song. La-la-di-dah-dahdi-dah." She clapped twice. "It's called 'The Mexican Hat Dance.'"

Callie raised an eyebrow. She pointed to the map. "Like this town. Mexican Hat."

Emma's focus zoomed in on the tiny dot on the map. The San Juan River etched a path near the town of Mexican Hat.

The music inside her head went silent as she remembered the end of her vision with dozens of sombreros tossed in the air. Mexican Hat. This was the clue she'd been waiting for. Her vision had been important after all. The mariachi song pointed the next step on the path to finding Aspen. "I need to go there."

The receptionist Emma had met at the front desk strode into the room. "I got the call from Bree," she announced. "The tribal elders will allow a CSI team to process Watts's house. You should leave right away."

Immediately, they went into action. Finding Sherman Watts was the number one priority.

THOUGH MIGUEL WAS ITCHING to get his hands on the evidence he was sure they'd find at Watts's house, Emma came first. He drove her car back toward her house. "Are you sure you don't want me to stay with you?"

"It won't be easy, but I can force myself to wait until you come home." As an afterthought, she said, "I'll save you a space on my bed."

Condoms, he remembered. He needed more condoms. "You'll be safe with Dylan."

"When you come back to me tonight, we might want to take some risks."

She leaned toward him, as far as her seat belt would allow, and stroked his jaw. When her thumb traced the line of his lips, he caught hold of her hand and kissed her palm. "You have risky business in mind?"

"Dangerous liaisons." Her voice was husky. "I've never felt like this before. I want to throw caution to the wind, to storm forth and conquer the world."

"Making love doesn't mean you've turned into a super-hero, Emma."

"Really?" She pulled her hand back. "I'm not invincible?"

"Not likely."

"And I can't fly? Except in the metaphorical sense."

"Metaphors?"

"My heart takes flight. Fly me to the moon. Be the wind beneath my wings." She heaved a sigh. "All those romantic song lyrics. I never understood them until now."

"Speaking of songs…"

"Mexican Hat," she said. "As soon as Callie pointed it out on the map, I saw the connection to my vision. All those sombreros must mean something. We need to go to Mexi-can Hat."

"Tomorrow," he promised.

"I'm not sure I can wait." She fidgeted in her seat. "But it's important for you to go to Watts's house on the rez. He's the best link we have to Aspen, and I want the best person handling the evidence. That means you."

"You just saw the crime lab in action. They're all good."

"But you're the best. Everyone else defers to you when it comes to crime scene evidence. Even Callie."

Without being too cocky, he knew she was right. In addition to gathering evidence, he had learned—through study and experience—how to take an overview of the scene. The application of inductive and deductive logic showed him where to look and what was significant.

He turned onto her street. "In case you need your car, I'll take my bike to the rez. It's parked in your driveway."

"By the time you get there, it'll be dark. Is it safe to ride your motorcycle at night?"

"I'll be fine."

As soon as he parked her car at the curb in front of her house, she unsnapped her seat belt and kissed him. Her mouth pressed hard. He pulled her onto his lap, wedged against the steering wheel. Her hair brushed his cheek, and he smelled the scent of her shampoo—fragrant as a night-blooming flower.

When they separated, his heart was beating faster. "I almost forgot what it was like to make out in a car."

"What's it like?"

"Uncomfortable."

Holding her, he gazed through the windshield. Daylight was fading. He needed to get moving, get to the scene. But he longed to stay here with her, to make love until dawn. "I'll miss you, *querida*."

"What will happen," she asked, "after we find Aspen and all the thugs are in jail?"

"Fiesta?"

"When you no longer need to stay with me as a bodyguard, what will you do?"

He wasn't about to plan the rest of their life in the two minutes that it took for him to walk from her car to his Harley. "Emma, this is a talk that needs more time than we have."

"Just wondering," she said.

She looked away from him. Was she hurt? *Dios mio*, that was the last thing he wanted. "I need to go."

She followed him to the Harley for another long, lingering kiss. Then she stepped back. "Be careful, Miguel."

He cranked the motor and flipped down the visor on his helmet. As he powered into the street, he looked back at Emma standing in front of her house. The wave of her hand tugged at his heart. He never wanted to leave her.

Logic told him that he would never find another woman like her. *Te amo, Emma.*

## Chapter Nineteen

Emma turned on her headlights as she drove east through the settling dusk. She lowered the driver's-side window halfway, and the evening breeze whisked across her face. Hoping to drown out the insistent mariachi music that still played inside her head, she reached for the buttons on the radio. Instead of the Mozart she usually played for the baby, she tuned to the oldies station.

The song on the radio made her grin. An old Frank Sinatra hit. Vincent Del Gardo would have loved this music. She sang along with the classic "My Way."

Her way. That was where she was headed. Her way.

Following her own path, even though she was pretty sure Miguel wouldn't approve. When he'd dropped her off, he'd expected her to march inside the house, lock the doors and stay there. He'd promised to take her to Mexican Hat tomorrow.

But she couldn't wait. In the crime lab, when she'd figured out the meaning of her fiesta vision, she knew that she had to follow that lead as soon as possible. Between her visions and Miguel's evidence, they were close to finding Aspen. Only inches away. With one final clue, the mystery of her cousin's disappearance would be solved.

Glancing to her right, Emma saw Grandma Quinn sitting in the passenger seat. "Go home, Emma."

"Why should I?"

"Because I said so." Grandma's voice was thin but firm. "You shouldn't be out here by yourself."

Since childhood, Grandma Quinn had watched over her like a guardian angel. Emma took her warnings seriously, but it wasn't as if she was plunging forward with no regard for her own safety. "I'm only going to look around at Mexican Hat. I have no intention of getting out of the car."

"Not even if you're led toward Aspen?"

Of course, that was what Emma hoped for. The best possible scenario would be for Julie Grainger to show up and point the way. "I won't rush in. I'll call for help."

"Tomorrow is soon enough."

"Then why was I given this vision?" She was so close to finding Aspen. "Can you tell me if she's there? Is Aspen in Mexican Hat?"

"This isn't like you, Emma. You're usually such a sensible girl."

She pulled onto the shoulder of the road and let the car behind her pass. In her encounters with her grandma, she tried to be respectful. Literally, she owed Grandma Quinn her life. "Please tell me. Will I find my cousin in Mexican Hat?"

"You know better than to ask. I'm not a fortune teller, dear." Her outline softened. "I want you to have all the happiness you deserve."

Emma remained adamant. "Aspen is there, isn't she? You can't deny it."

"Go home," Grandma Quinn repeated. "Be safe."

Then she vanished.

An old pickup truck rumbled by. This wasn't a busy road, but there was a fairly steady stream of traffic. Nobody would attack her with all these witnesses; she ought to be safe.

The cell phone in her purse rang. Caller ID showed it was Miguel. Explaining herself to him would be far more difficult than dealing with Grandma Quinn. Reluctantly, she answered.

"Dylan called," he said. "It seems that you never made it into the house. He stood at the front window and watched you get in your car and drive away."

She tried to change the subject. "How was his afternoon of babysitting?"

"Where the hell are you, Emma?"

"Going to Mexican Hat."

"Not anymore. Turn the car around and go home."

"I'm not being reckless," she said. "Bridger was sighted near Telluride. He's probably on his way back to Vegas. In any case, he's far away from me."

"What about Sherman Watts? And Boyd Perkins?"

"They're both on the run for their lives. Nobody has seen Perkins in days. By now, Watts knows he's the target of a manhunt. Why would either of them bother with me?"

There was a pause as Miguel considered her words. "I don't know."

"You see? No need for worry. I'm only going to drive through Mexican Hat near the San Juan River. In my first vision, I saw a river."

"You also saw someone who wanted to kill you."

A shudder went through her. She hadn't forgotten the faceless man with a knife. "He was chasing me. If I don't get out of the car, that can't happen. I'll be safe."

She couldn't say the words that poised on the tip of her tongue, couldn't bring herself to tell him that she probably didn't need a bodyguard anymore.

Parked at the edge of the road, she watched as headlights approached and drove on.

Earlier, when she'd asked him what would happen when

his presence wasn't necessary to keep her safe, she'd made a mistake. She had no right to push him or make inappropriate demands. Just because they'd made love, it didn't mean they were going to be together forever. Plenty of women—sophisticated women—were able to have sex with a man, then say *adios*. At least, that was what Emma had heard. She'd read about casual sex in novels. Seen it in movies.

But there was nothing casual about her feelings for Miguel. She wanted him with a passion that was bigger and more powerful than an avalanche. But she couldn't force him to feel the same way about her.

"Where are you?" he repeated. "On what route?"

"Why do you want to know?"

"I'll join you, *querida*. I think you need a motorcycle escort through Mexican Hat."

Her heart took a happy leap. She'd love to have him with her, but she didn't want to tear him away from his investigation. "I'm all right, Miguel. Stay where you are."

"I'll find you."

Before she could object, he disconnected the call.

AFTER A QUICK EXPLANATION to Callie, Miguel remapped his route. Locating Emma wouldn't be difficult; there weren't that many roads that went through Mexican Hat near the river.

Though her rationale about being safe made a certain amount of sense, she wasn't acting on logic. Emma was following her feelings. *That's what she did.* Her actions were directed by ghosts and emotions. *That's why she needed him.*

He brought reality and common sense to her life. He wouldn't take any chances with her safety, not even if the odds were a hundred to one. She meant too much to him.

*Stubborn woman.* He wheeled around on his Harley. Fortunately, Mexican Hat wasn't far from the rez. He might even get there before she did.

APPROACHING THE RIVER, Emma slowed her car. The traffic was almost nonexistent. A desolate night had descended, sprinkling stars across the black velvet skies. In the distance, she saw the lights from the town of Mexican Hat, but there were no houses nearby. On one side of the road were open fields leading toward forests and jagged cliffs. On the other was the river—about forty yards away and down an incline.

She pulled off and parked in a wide area overlooking the river. Gravel crunched under her tires. She'd promised not to leave the car, but there was no rule against lowering the window. She turned off her engine and listened to the rush of cold, white water. A chill slid down her spine.

Among the cottonwoods near the edge of the river, she saw the figure of a woman. Aspen? Was she here? Anticipation mixed with dread as Emma watched the ethereal figure approach. A spirit. If this woman was Aspen, it meant her cousin was dead.

In a logical sense, Aspen's death was likely. Why else would she be gone for so long? Why else abandon her baby? For the first time since this investigation started, Emma allowed herself to consider the horrible possibility of her cousin's death. She didn't want it to be true, didn't want to step out of her car and find Aspen's body.

Hands gripping the steering wheel, she watched as the woman came closer. Her FBI jacket caught on the breeze. Julie Grainger. Emma whispered her name.

A vision flashed before her eyes. Julie in a life-and-death struggle, fighting off two men.

Emma blinked and the vision was gone. Julie came closer. The wind tossed her hair. Moonlight shone on her pale face.

Purposefully, Emma closed her eyes. She needed to know what had happened, needed to see. Julie's lifeless body was being dragged across dirt and rocks.

Then she saw Aspen. Like Emma, Aspen watched as the men disposed of Julie's body.

The vision dissipated. When Emma looked up, she saw Julie striding closer. Even in death, she was strong and full of purpose. She spoke one word. "Witness."

Aspen had been a witness.

Julie disappeared into the night, leaving Emma shaking with anger and regret. Finally, she knew how Aspen was connected to Del Gardo and these other crimes. She knew why Aspen had been attacked. Her cousin had done nothing wrong. Aspen had merely been in the wrong place at the wrong time. She'd seen something she shouldn't have seen. And she'd paid the price for her bad luck.

But was she dead? Emma wished that Miguel was here; he could translate her vision into logic. When he was with her, she felt grounded and safe. She needed him. Alone, she had too many questions and too few answers.

Aspen's abandoned car with Jack in the backseat had been found far away from this place. Why had she come here?

Mexican Hat was close to the rez. Had Aspen been trying to get back home?

"Julie," Emma whispered, "come back."

She needed more information. Her hand rested on the door latch. Julie had come from those trees by the river. Should she go there?

This area was not well-traveled. It had been several minutes since any cars passed the overlook where she was parked. She glanced toward the road and saw the outline of a pickup truck pulled off on the shoulder about twenty yards behind her. Its lights were off.

She didn't remember passing a parked truck before she pulled off which meant that he must have been following her. But she hadn't seen his headlights. She remembered the careful way Bridger had kept his distance when he followed them from the reservation. This couldn't be him. He drove an SUV, not a truck. And he'd been sighted in Telluride, far away from Kenner City…unless he'd turned around and come back…unless the state patrol had made a mistake in identifying his vehicle.

This was enough investigation for tonight. She cranked the key in the ignition.

Before she could back up and pull away, the truck was behind her. Its lights were still off. She tried to drive forward, making a sharp turn. The nose of the vehicle tapped her bumper. She jolted.

The only escape route was straight ahead. Her foot jammed down on the accelerator and the engine whined. She drove off the gravel overlook onto the moist earth. Her car wasn't made for off-road driving. Her undercarriage crashed over rocks and ditches.

She tried to turn, but her steering wheel wouldn't respond. Forward momentum carried her toward the trees at the river's edge. She jammed on the brake but couldn't stop. Her car wasn't going fast. Just fast enough to keep rolling. Her front bumper smacked the trunk of a cottonwood.

The impact was painful. The air bag exploded in her face.

Frantic, Emma fought the bag. Her car was dead. Her window was still open. If she sat here, he'd grab her.

Struggling, she stumbled out of her car. Pain shot up her leg from her ankle. She must have injured herself when she hit the tree. No time to think about that now. She lurched forward.

To her right, the river roared. The bare branches of trees rattled in the wind. Gritting her teeth, she forced herself to run. To run for her life.

Adrenaline surged through her body, giving her much-needed strength. If she got back to the road, there might be another car. She might find someone to help her.

"Help me," she cried out. "Someone help me."

She turned and saw the dark figure of a man coming after her—moving fast while she was clumsy. Her ankle must be sprained. Her whole leg felt numb. Still, she dodged around a clump of sagebrush.

Her pursuer came closer. She could hear him.

She had no way to fight him off. No gun. No weapon.

His hand gripped her arm. He spun her around.

Off balance, she fell to the earth. Her bare hands scraped against the rocks.

He loomed over her. Like her vision. But she clearly saw his face, and she recognized Sherman Watts from the photographs.

"Where is she?" he demanded.

He must be talking about Aspen. Emma took a breath, hoping to calm her racing pulse. The only way she'd survive was to outsmart him, convince him that he was better off keeping her alive.

She sat up, brushed the dirt off her arms and tried to sound like she was in control. "Why were you following me?"

Beneath the flat brim of his hat, his dark eyes glittered in the moonlight like hot coals. "Following you?"

"That's right."

She tried to sound confident, but she feared this encounter would not turn out well. Dealing with Bridger, she'd been able to engage his intelligence, to mess with his head. Watts wasn't a thinking man. She could smell the cheap whiskey on his breath.

"Where is she?" he demanded.

"You must have been following me."

"You got it wrong, bitch. You came to me."

To Mexican Hat. Her vision had led her into a trap. "Why are you here?"

"I don't have to answer any damn questions from you."

He yanked her to her feet. Her ankle throbbed, and she let out a yip.

"You're hurt." His lip curled in an ugly sneer.

"My ankle." She supported her weight on her other leg. "I think it's sprained."

He shook her. "You came here to meet your cousin. Tell me where the hell she's hiding."

"I don't know."

He drew back his foot and kicked her injured ankle.

She hated herself for whimpering, but the pain was so intense that she felt light-headed.

"Where is she?" he demanded. "I should have killed her when I dumped her here. I never thought she'd survive in the river. But nobody found her body."

"You showed mercy," Emma said. "That was wise. You don't want to kill a daughter of your tribe."

"Mercy." He scoffed. "I won't make that mistake again."

He drew a hunting knife from a sheath fastened to his belt. The moonlight gleamed on the blade. "Where is she?"

Playing for time, Emma bluffed. "I have to take you there. I can't tell you exactly where it is. I have to show you."

He stroked the flat of the blade against her cheek. "If you lie, you die."

"It's the truth," she said desperately. "I swear."

A gunshot exploded through the night.

Sherman Watts shoved her away, and she fell to the

ground. She curled into a ball to ward off any blow. Her arms covered her head.

Another shot.

Watts took off running like the coward he was.

Emma stayed where she was, breathing in heavy gasps. She'd been close to death, almost a victim. Waves of pain washed over her. Pain and relief.

Miguel must be coming to her rescue. He had to be the person who'd fired the shots.

She heard him tromping through the sage, coming closer. Thank God, he hadn't listened when she told him to stay at the other scene. Thank God, he'd come for her.

She opened her eyes and looked up into the face of Hank Bridger. This nightmare wasn't over.

## Chapter Twenty

On his Harley, Miguel rode slowly along the road that bordered the San Juan outside Mexican Hat. He hoped that Emma had already made this drive and was safely on her way back to the house, but he needed to be sure before he returned to his forensic team on the rez.

Pulling off on a graveled overlook—the only good stopping place along this stretch—he took out his cell phone and speed dialed her number. All he heard was a lonely buzz before it switched over to her voice mail.

Annoyed, he snapped the phone closed. She was probably right in assuming there was no reason for worry. Chasing after her was an overreaction on his part.

But what if he was right?

In the light from the waning moon, he noticed tire tracks gouged in the gravel. He dismounted from his bike to take a closer look. These were recent tracks, not eroded by wind or weather.

Miguel stepped back to get a better perspective. He'd done this sort of crime scene investigation dozens of time, reconstructing an accident. Based on skid marks and tire tracks, he could see that there were two vehicles. One had a wider base, probably a truck, and it had come too close to the first vehicle. There was a possible collision at slow speed, less than ten miles per hour. The smaller car, the one in front, had driven over the edge of the overlook and across the rutted landscape.

His gaze followed the path that car had taken. He squinted through the night. About twenty-five yards away was Emma's car. She'd run headlong into a tree.

He knew this wasn't an accident. The truck had forced her off the road. Someone had been chasing her.

Grabbing his flashlight, Miguel ran down the incline toward the river. His heart beat so fast that he thought it would jump out of his chest. He reached the car in seconds.

The front bumper had crumpled on impact. Her air bag had deployed. The driver's-side door hung open. She was gone.

"Emma," he called out. "Emma, where are you?"

He listened hard, hoping to hear her voice over the rush of the river and the wind.

Inside his head, his thoughts careened. A few days ago, he hadn't even known her name. Now, she was everything to him. She was his future. The only woman he ever wanted to be with. He never should have left her alone, not for one minute.

The Chimayo medal he wore around his neck burned against his skin. He held the silver disk between his thumb and forefinger, absorbing the words on the back: Protect and Heal. That was his mission. He must find Emma. Protect her.

He could do this. The evidence was here. All he needed to do was process the clues correctly.

The beam of his flashlight followed the tire tracks that led from the overlook to this tree. Shrubs lay flattened. There were deep ruts where her tires had churned on the rugged soil. She'd been trying to drive fast, but the terrain was too much for her little car. She'd lost control and hit the tree.

His attention turned to the car interior. Her purse sat on

the passenger seat. In the back was Jack's baby seat. Nothing inside the car resembled a clue.

He focused on the ground beside the car, trying to see which way she'd gone. He saw a partial print from her purple sneaker. Then another. She'd been on her toes, running. Running for her life.

Miguel seldom feared for his own safety. When faced with danger, his mind became calm and even more rational than usual. He thought ahead, trusted himself to do what needed to be done.

But when he thought of Emma—frightened and alone— his gut clenched. His ability to reason was replaced by fierce emotion. Fear surged inside him. Panic at the edge of a scream. He feared for her.

"No." He stood upright and inhaled a steady breath.

Overhead, the stars scattered across the night sky. After Teresa died, he imagined her in heaven, being a distant star that would guide him. He couldn't lose Emma, too. Fate couldn't be so cruel. *Think,* vato. *Think and you will find her.*

Concentrating on the trail she'd left as she ran, he came to an area where the ground was more disturbed. Someone had fallen here. He squatted down and carefully inspected the ground with his flashlight. There had been a struggle. *Emma,* mi amor, *you fought hard.*

Then he saw the boot print—size thirteen, square-toed, custom made. Hank Bridger's boot.

He remembered what Emma had said at the lab. *Bridger and the tunnels.* They went together.

He took out his cell phone, called for backup.

Miguel knew where Emma had gone.

BARELY CONSCIOUS, Emma slumped in the passenger seat beside Hank Bridger. He'd been considerate enough to fasten her seat belt, but her hands were cuffed in front of her. Her wrists chafed. When she moved, her ankle throbbed.

"You awake?" Bridger growled.

It might be safer to pretend that she was unconscious, but she was too exhausted to come up with a clever plan. Unrelenting fear had sapped her strength and intelligence. "Where are we going?"

"Where you told me," he said. "The place where Del Gardo died."

"The mine tunnels."

Was he still searching for the treasure? Surely, he knew that the crime lab had been all over Del Gardo's hideout.

"You told me," Bridger repeated, "that you were the only one who knew where to look. Del Gardo's ghost showed you the way."

Emma truly didn't remember telling him anything, much less spinning a fantastic yarn about how she could find the treasure when no one else could. Nor could she recall how she'd gotten from the field by the river to his car.

When she'd looked up and seen Bridger instead of Miguel, her hopes shattered. She'd been overwhelmed by a dread certainty that she would never get out of this alive. She'd never see Miguel again, never know what they might have shared together.

Knowing she had nothing to lose, she asked, "How do you know where Del Gardo died?"

He turned to her and smiled—wolflike, predatory. "I think you know that answer."

"You killed him. And those other people, too."

"You're too smart for your own good, Miss Emma." He maneuvered onto the turn below Griffin's house. "When you said their names, my first plan was to cut my losses and head back to Vegas. I talked to my lawyer. He said evidence from a medium would never be allowed in court."

"He's right. No one would believe me."

"Your testimony carries even less weight than circumstantial evidence." He drove slowly on the narrow road. She noticed that he wore black driving gloves, leaving no fingerprints. "But I changed my mind."

"Why?"

"I like a sure bet. If I eliminate you, the proof is gone. As a bonus, you can show me where to find Del Gardo's millions."

"Why should I? What's in it for me?"

He stopped at almost the exact same place she and Miguel had parked when they were following her hunch. "We might be able to work out a deal. I'd give you ten percent to pay for your silence."

"Only ten? That's not much of an incentive."

He unsnapped her seat belt and grabbed the front of her jacket, pulling her close to his face. "Ten percent. And I don't cut out your tongue."

She swallowed hard. "I have a better deal. A really sure thing."

"I'm listening."

"You said that Del Gardo owed you a hundred thousand. I'll pay you that much if you take me home."

His gaze turned blank. Talking about finance, he put on a poker face. "If this is a bluff—"

"It's not," she said desperately.

"How would a mouse like you come up with that kind of dough?"

"I make a lot of money and my needs are simple. My profits are all in the bank. All I have to do is talk to my financial advisor."

"You? You have a financial advisor?"

"It's true." When she'd lied to Bridger about the Manitou, he'd readily believed her. Now, she was telling the truth, and he was suspicious. "You can call my accountant. He'll tell you."

He leaned back in his seat. "Even if you're not shining me on, why would I make that deal? You've seen things that would put me in jail."

"Nobody will believe me. You said it yourself. My visions don't count for a damn thing in a court of law."

He shoved open his car door and got out.

Terror crashed through her. A suppressed sob escaped her lips. She was going to die.

The passenger's-side door whipped open. Roughly, he pulled her out. When her foot hit the gravel road, she winced in pain.

"Please." She gasped. "I'll pay you."

"Why would I settle for your money when I can have Del Gardo's millions?"

"Getting my money is easy. Just a phone call." She gestured with her cuffed hands. "A transfer of funds. From my account to yours."

"And that might be a reason to keep you alive until morning when the banks are open." He shoved her shoulder. "For now, I want Del Gardo's treasure. Show me where it is."

She hobbled forward.

"Let's go. Move it."

She stumbled. "I have a sprained ankle. I can't go any faster. Maybe if you take off the handcuffs."

He whirled her around. Using a key, he unfastened the cuffs that bound her wrists together.

With her hands free, there might be something she could do to protect herself. If she could get her hands on something she could use as a weapon. A rock. A tree branch.

She studied the huge man in the fringed jacket, taking his measure. There was no way to overcome him.

And he held a gun. His voice was low and calm. "Make no mistake, Miss Emma. If you try anything cute, I will hurt you."

To illustrate, he delivered a glancing blow to her right temple. The burst of pain made her gasp. When she touched the spot, she felt wet blood.

A sudden certainty hit her. "This is what happened when you killed Del Gardo."

"That's right." He nudged her arm with the barrel of his gun. "Start moving."

She limped uphill toward the three trees. "You brought him here. He promised to lead you to the treasure."

"He took some convincing."

She remembered the coroner's report. Del Gardo had been beaten before he was shot. "Then what happened?"

"He started running. I had to chase after him. His old-man disguise tricked me. I forgot how strong he was."

Emma dragged herself forward, putting as little weight on her sprained ankle as she could. "But he was taking you toward the money. Why did you kill him?"

"He had a rifle stashed over by that rock. When I saw the gun, I thought he brought me here as a ruse. So he could get to his weapon."

"You were so close," she said, thinking of the tunnels.

"The bastard was never going to hand over the money. I had to kill him. Or be killed."

But the treasure might actually be here. She couldn't imagine how Bobby and Ava could have overlooked millions of dollars hidden in the caves. But it was possible. Del Gardo could have changed his cash into diamonds or gold coins. When she first saw him, he was digging up coins.

If she could find his stash, she might figure out a way to survive.

She heard a rustling in the trees and glanced in that

direction. For an instant, she thought she saw the shape of a man. Now would be a good time for a vision. "Del Gardo," she whispered.

She needed his ghost, needed him to show her the way.

They had reached the place where she'd found his body. Bridger tore aside the yellow crime scene tape with a gloved hand. "Keep going," he growled.

She heard the hum of a motorcycle. *Miguel.* Her fear trebled. She'd rather die than have anything happened to Miguel. But if she died, Jack would have no one. *Oh, Miguel.*

"Your boyfriend," Bridger said. "I hate to shoot a cop, but I will. Keep moving."

Struggling, she pulled herself up the steep incline toward the entrance to the mine shaft.

The sound of the motorcycle went dead. How was she going to get free? She peered into the rustling trees. Somebody had to help her.

"How much farther?" Bridger demanded.

"Not much." She paused, catching her breath. "This is a hard climb."

"Keep going."

She knew what he wanted. If they made it to the ledge, he'd have an advantage. He could look down on anyone approaching. Taking aim at Miguel would be easier.

And she couldn't let that happen.

Glancing over her shoulder, she saw Bridger below her. His eyes cast downward, picking out careful steps on the loose dirt of ancient mine tailings. She couldn't let him get his footing. He had to be stopped. This was her best chance.

She gathered her strength. Using her body as a missile, she launched herself into his huge, barrel chest. Off balance, they both tumbled down the hill to the spot where he'd killed Del Gardo.

Emma tried to move, but she couldn't.

Bridger grabbed for her.

"Don't move," a voice shouted through the trees. She knew that voice. Sheriff Martinez.

"You're surrounded," came another shout from another direction.

"Let her go." It was Miguel. He'd come for her. He'd arranged this trap.

As she watched, Bridger leaped to his feet. He raised his gun. The barrel pointed directly at her. Horrified, she watched. Time slowed. Seconds passed like hours as she waited for death.

When the first gunshot rang out, he stumbled. Other shots followed in rapid succession.

Bridger fell to the ground, twitched once and went still.

Miguel came to her, gathered her into his arms. She rested her head against his chest, too weak to embrace him.

"You're all right, Emma. You're going to be all right."

"How did this happen? How did you—"

"Logic, *querida.* I found your car. I saw Bridger's boot print, and I remembered what you said about the tunnels."

"But how—"

"I called for backup. I'm the smart twin, remember?"

She lifted her chin. His smile was the most wonderful sight she'd ever seen. "You're brilliant."

"Martinez and his men had enough time to set up an ambush before you got here."

She counted three other men besides Martinez. The sheriff felt for a pulse in Bridger's neck. Then, he shook his head. The big man was dead.

"Died with his boots on," Martinez said.

She nestled against Miguel. "I never should have taken off by myself."

"I'll never leave you alone again. I want to be with you for all time. Even when you don't need a bodyguard. I love you, Emma."

"In Spanish?"

*"Te quiero. Te amo."*

"And I love you, Miguel. With all my heart."

# *Epilogue*

Some days later, Miguel's love for Emma had grown deeper. He'd put down roots, moving his belongings into her house. More important, he'd taken up permanent residence in her bed, where she continued to amaze him with the intensity of her passion. Ever since she abandoned her virginity, she couldn't get enough of lovemaking. *Sí,* he was a lucky man.

He leaned over on the sofa and gave her a little kiss on the forehead, just below the bandage that covered the spot where Bridger struck her.

"Lovebirds," his brother muttered.

Dylan sat in the rocking chair, feeding a bottle to the baby. It seemed that he couldn't get enough of Jack. Since the day he'd spent babysitting, he had bonded with the motherless child.

"Maybe," Emma said, "if you'd stop being so macho, you might find a woman who could put up with you."

"I have plenty of *chicas,*" Dylan said.

But love was different. Deep and powerful and strong. Miguel was glad he'd been patient enough to wait for Emma to come into his life.

When she shifted her weight, he asked, "How's the ankle?"

"Almost better. I'm feeling good enough to hobble around in the kitchen and make dinner tonight."

"No need, *querida.*" He'd tasted her cooking. He was the better chef. "I like making food for you."

Dylan groaned. "I can't stand all this lovey-dovey goop. Can we talk about something important? Like Sherman Watts?"

"Have they found him?"

"Not yet, but the search is—"

When Emma stood, Miguel was at her elbow. "Do you need something?"

"I'm perfectly capable of walking to the kitchen," she assured him. "You two can talk. I have nothing to say about Watts."

As soon as she left the room, Dylan lowered his voice. "Unless we find Watts, I'm afraid we'll never locate Aspen. We've searched all over Mexican Hat. There's no sign of her."

"Watts doesn't know where she is. He's looking for her, too."

"How could she vanish?" Dylan looked down at the baby in his arms. "Where the hell is your mama?"

"Maybe somewhere on the rez. Have you made your peace with Bree?"

"No *problemo,*" Dylan said. "I apologized. She accepted."

"So you're back in everybody's good graces."

Dylan's late-night raid on Watts's house hadn't really done any harm. The forensic investigation at his place hadn't turned up anything of significance.

When Emma came back into the living room carrying a bottle of water, she halted. Standing very still, her blue eyes focused on a spot near the front door.

Miguel recognized what was happening. She was seeing

one of her ghosts. He rose from the sofa and went toward her. "What is it, Emma? What do you see?"

A beautiful smile broke across her face. Excitedly, she said, "We'll find her. I know where Aspen is…."

\* \* \* \* \*

*Will the truth about Julie Grainger's*
*murder ever be revealed?*
*Find out next month in Rita Herren's*
*COLLECTING EVIDENCE,*
*as* Kenner County Crime Unit
*continues in Harlequin Intrigue!*

*Celebrate 60 years of pure
reading pleasure with Harlequin®!*

*Step back in time and enjoy a
sneak preview of an exciting anthology
from Harlequin® Historical with*
THE DIAMONDS OF WELBOURNE MANOR.

This compelling anthology features three stories about
the outrageous Fitzmanning sisters. Meet Annalise,
who is never at a loss for words… But that can change
with an unexpected encounter in the forest.

*Available May 2009
from Harlequin® Historical.*

"I'm the illegitimate daughter of notoriously scandalous parents, Mr. Milford. Candidates for my hand are unlikely to be lining up at the gates."

"Don't be so quick to discount your charms, my dear. Or the charm of your substantial dowry. Or even your brothers' influence. There are as many reasons to marry as there are marriages."

Annalise snorted. "Oh, yes. Perhaps I shall marry for dynastic reasons, or perhaps for property or influence. After all, a loveless, practical marriage worked out so well for my mother."

"Well, you've routed me on that one. I can think of no suitable rejoinder." Ned rose to his feet and extended his hand. "And since that is the case, let me be the first to wish you a long and happy spinsterhood."

Her mouth gaped open. And then she laughed.

And he froze.

This was the first time, Ned realized. The first time he'd seen her eyes light up and her mouth curl. The first time he'd witnessed her features melded together in glorious accord to produce exquisite beauty.

Unbelievable what a change came over her face. Unheard of what effect her throaty, rasping laughter had on his body. It pounded a beat upon his ear, quickly taken up by his pulse. It echoed through him, finally residing in his stirring nether regions.

So easily she did it, awakened these sensations within him—without any apparent effort at all. And she had called him potentially dangerous? Clearly the intelligent thing for him to do would be to steer clear, to leave her to the tender ministrations of Lord Peter Blackthorne.

"You were right." She smiled up at him as she took his hand and climbed to her feet. "I do feel better."

Ah, well. When had he ever chosen the intelligent path?

He did not relinquish her hand. He used it to pull her in, close enough that he could feel the warmth of her. "At the risk of repeating Lord Peter's mistake and anticipating too much—may I ask if you'll be my partner in battledore tomorrow?"

Her smiled dimmed. Her breath came a little faster. His own had gone shallow, as if he'd just run a race—and lost. He ran his gaze over the appealing lift of her brow and the curious angle of her chin. His index finger twitched.

"I should like that," she said.

His finger trembled again and he lifted it, traced the pink and tender shell of her ear, the unique sweep of her jaw. Her pulse leaped beneath her skin, triggering his own. Slowly he tilted her chin up, waiting for her to object, to step back, to slap his hand away.

She did none of those eminently sensible things. Which left him free to do the entirely impractical thing.

Baby soft, the skin of her lips. Her whole body trembled when he touched her there.

He leaned in. Her eyes closed, even as she stood straight against him, strung as tight as a bow. He pressed his mouth to hers. It was a soft kiss, sweet and chaste. And yet he was hot and hard and as ready as he'd ever been in his life.

She drew back a little. Sighed. Their breath mingled a moment before she slowly backed away.

"Oh," she breathed. Her dark eyes were full of wonder and something that looked like fear. He took a step toward her, but she only shook her head. His outstretched hand fell to his side as she turned to disappear into the wood. This was the first time, Ned realized. The first time, since he'd come to the house party at Welbourne Manor, that he'd seen her eyes light up.

\* \* \* \* \*

*Follow Ned and Annalise's story in May 2009 in*
*THE DIAMONDS OF WELBOURNE MANOR.*
*Available May 2009 from Harlequin® Historical.*

*Available in the series romance section,*
*or in the historical romance section,*
*wherever books are sold.*

We'll be spotlighting a different series every month
throughout 2009 to celebrate our 60th anniversary.

### Look for Harlequin®
### American Romance® in June!

Join us for a year-long celebration of the rugged
American male! From cops to cowboys—
Men Made in America has the hero
you've been dreaming about!

Look for

# The Chief Ranger

### by Rebecca Winters, on sale in June!

| | |
|---|---|
| *Bachelor CEO* by Michele Dunaway | July |
| *The Rodeo Rider* by Roxann Delaney | August |
| *Doctor Daddy* by Jacqueline Diamond | September |

**www.eHarlequin.com**     HARBPA09

# SPECIAL EDITION

**FROM *USA TODAY* BESTSELLING AUTHOR**

# MARIE FERRARELLA

## THE ALASKANS

## LOVING THE RIGHT BROTHER

When tragedy struck, Irena Yovich headed
back to Alaska to console her ex-boyfriend's
family. While there she began seeing his brother,
Brody Hayes, in a very different light. Things
were about to really heat up. Had she fallen
for the wrong brother?

*Available in June
wherever books are sold.*

# REQUEST YOUR FREE BOOKS!

## 2 FREE NOVELS PLUS 2 FREE GIFTS!

**HARLEQUIN®**

# INTRIGUE®

## Breathtaking Romantic Suspense

**YES!** Please send me 2 FREE Harlequin Intrigue® novels and my 2 FREE gifts (gifts are worth about $10). After receiving them, if I don't wish to receive any more books, I can return the shipping statement marked "cancel." If I don't cancel, I will receive 6 brand-new novels every month and be billed just $4.24 per book in the U.S. or $4.99 per book in Canada. That's a savings of close to 15% off the cover price! It's quite a bargain! Shipping and handling is just 25¢ per book*. I understand that accepting the 2 free books and gifts places me under no obligation to buy anything. I can always return a shipment and cancel at any time. Even if I never buy another book from Harlequin, the two free books and gifts are mine to keep forever.

182 HDN EEZ7  382 HDN EEZK

| Name | (PLEASE PRINT) | |
|---|---|---|
| Address | | Apt. # |
| City | State/Prov. | Zip/Postal Code |

Signature (if under 18, a parent or guardian must sign)

### Mail to the **Harlequin Reader Service:**
**IN U.S.A.:** P.O. Box 1867, Buffalo, NY 14240-1867
**IN CANADA:** P.O. Box 609, Fort Erie, Ontario L2A 5X3

Not valid to current subscribers of Harlequin Intrigue books.

**Are you a current subscriber of Harlequin Intrigue books
and want to receive the larger-print edition?
Call 1-800-873-8635 today!**

\* Terms and prices subject to change without notice. Prices do not include applicable taxes. Sales tax applicable in N.Y. Canadian residents will be charged applicable provincial taxes and GST. Offer not valid in Quebec. This offer is limited to one order per household. All orders subject to approval. Credit or debit balances in a customer's account(s) may be offset by any other outstanding balance owed by or to the customer. Please allow 4 to 6 weeks for delivery. Offer available while quantities last.

**Your Privacy:** Harlequin is committed to protecting your privacy. Our Privacy Policy is available online at www.eHarlequin.com or upon request from the Reader Service. From time to time we make our lists of customers available to reputable third parties who may have a product or service of interest to you. If you would prefer we not share your name and address, please check here. ☐

HI09

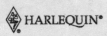